Spark of Suspicion

On the far side of the marina, a man stood on the deck of his boat. He watched the local officials gather on the speakers' platform. This was the crowd he was after. He smiled as the town supervisor climbed the steps to the platform. The town supervisor moved to the front, ready to address the crowd.

The time for action had come. The man's smile disappeared. He stared across Barmet Bay.

"Goodbye," the man said. "Goodbye, Bayport."

At exactly 10:00 P.M., he jabbed the deadly red button on his transmitter. . . .

The Hardy Boys Mystery Stories

#60 Mystery of the Samurai Sword
#61 The Pentagon Spy
#62 The Apeman's Secret
#63 The Mummy Case
#64 Mystery of Smugglers Cove
#65 The Stone Idol
#66 The Vanishing Thieves
#67 The Outlaw's Silver
#68 Deadly Chase
#69 The Four-headed Dragon
#70 The Infinity Clue
#71 Track of the Zombie
#72 The Voodoo Plot
#73 The Billion Dollar Ransom
#74 Tic-Tac-Terror
#75 Trapped at Sea
#76 Game Plan for Disaster
#77 The Crimson Flame
#78 Cave-in!
#79 Sky Sabotage
#80 The Roaring River Mystery
#81 The Demon's Den
#82 The Blackwing Puzzle
#83 The Swamp Monster
#84 Revenge of the Desert Phantom
#85 The Skyfire Puzzle
#86 The Mystery of the Silver Star
#87 Program for Destruction
#88 Tricky Business
#89 The Sky Blue Frame
#90 Danger on the Diamond
#91 Shield of Fear
#92 The Shadow Killers
#93 The Serpent's Tooth Mystery
#94 Breakdown in Axeblade
#95 Danger on the Air
#96 Wipeout
#97 Cast of Criminals
#98 Spark of Suspicion
#99 Dungeon of Doom
#100 The Secret of the Island Treasure
#101 The Money Hunt

Available from MINSTREL Books

THE HARDY BOYS® MYSTERY STORIES

98

The HARDY BOYS®

SPARK OF SUSPICION

FRANKLIN W. DIXON

PUBLISHED BY POCKET BOOKS

New York London Toronto Sydney Tokyo Singapore

This book is a work of fiction. Names, characters, places and incidents are either the product of the author's imagination or are used fictitiously. Any resemblance to actual events or locales or persons, living or dead, is entirely coincidental.

A MINSTREL PAPERBACK *ORIGINAL*

A Minstrel Book published by
POCKET BOOKS, a division of Simon & Schuster Inc.
1230 Avenue of the Americas, New York, NY 10020

Produced by Mega-Books of New York, Inc.

ISBN: 0-671-66304-6

First Minstrel Books printing October 1989

10 9 8 7 6 5 4 3 2

Printed in the U.S.A.

Contents

1.	*Barbary Blood*	*1*
2.	*Behind the Mystery Door*	*12*
3.	*Out of the Dark*	*22*
4.	*More Rumors of Sabotage*	*33*
5.	*A Talk with Anna Siegel*	*43*
6.	*Not Just Scare Tactics*	*52*
7.	*Trapped!*	*61*
8.	*I Read You Loud and Clear*	*72*
9.	*Stakeout*	*82*
10.	*Evidence on the Videotape*	*93*
11.	*Kevin Bailey, Suspect*	*106*
12.	*Collins Comes Clean*	*122*
13.	*Mad for Revenge*	*129*
14.	*Goodbye, Bayport*	*137*
15.	*Fireworks*	*145*

1 Barbary Blood

"That fuse is too short!" Joe Hardy protested as his older brother lit a match.

Frank Hardy's dark eyes sparked with annoyance. "We can't waste the time." He touched the match to the fuse. "Now! Start shooting!"

Behind them, a door opened, and their mother stepped out into the backyard. "Boys —what's going on?"

With a hiss and a whiz, the skyrocket ignited and shot into the sky, where it exploded with a loud *pop!*

"Did you get it, Joe?" Frank asked eagerly.

Joe's blond head leaned far back, still glued to the eyepiece of his video camera. "I think so. We'll just have to play it back and see. Let's—"

"Let's all head back to the kitchen and wash those dishes you left from breakfast," Mrs. Hardy said. "Then you can tell me what you're up to."

As Joe dried, Frank washed and explained the mysterious doings in the backyard. "We're on a special assignment for 'Good Morning, Bayport.' Besides our usual Crimestoppers bit, we're doing a piece on the Founders' Day fireworks show." He grinned. "What you saw out there was supposed to be our opener—if Joe caught it. We could only get hold of one rocket."

"That's not surprising, what with the big celebration only a week away," Mrs. Hardy said. "Fireworks must be hard to come by. Still, it's not every year a town turns three hundred years old. I guess everyone wants to light up the sky."

"Everyone except Frank and me," Joe said. "We'll be lighting up the television. This project is our baby. We'll be doing the whole thing—even the editing—ourselves."

Joe put the last plate into the kitchen cupboard. "Today we're taping at the Old Glory Fireworks Company factory. Their public relations department set everything up for us." He had a mischievous glint in his blue eyes as he dried his hands. "I wonder if they give out free samples."

Mrs. Hardy handed him the Minicam. "Stick with taking pictures," she said. "Fireworks can be dangerous."

"Don't worry, Mom," Frank said with a grin. "I'll keep Joe out of trouble."

Joe gave him a look. "Before we go out to the

Old Glory factory," he said, "let's stop off at the marina for some shots of the *Barbary Blood.*" He grinned at his mother. "I don't know why they bring in a pirate ship for Founders' Day. Makes it seem like the town's founders were pirates."

"The pirates came along much later—in 1728," Mrs. Hardy said. "The town brings in the ship to give the celebration a little pizzazz." She laughed. "When I was a little girl, that big black boat always used to frighten me."

"Well, wait till you see it this year," Frank said. "That's where they'll be launching the fireworks on Saturday night." He jumped from his chair and headed for the front door. "See you tonight, Mom."

"What time will you be home for dinner?" Mrs. Hardy called after them.

"About six o'clock, I guess," Frank said over his shoulder. Stepping outside, he nearly crashed into Joe, who was bent over something by the front door. Joe straightened up, a white envelope in his hand. On the outside was typed: "To Frank and Joe Hardy. Important!!!"

Frowning, Joe tore open the envelope. Inside was a piece of plain paper, folded in half. Joe unfolded it and read aloud:

"'If you really want a scoop for your TV show, find out who's going to blow up the Founders' Day celebration. It could be a real crowd-killer.'"

Joe stared at his brother. "Do you believe this?" he asked.

"Either it's a joke or a challenge," Frank said. "Whoever sent it picked the right people."

Joe and Frank often helped their detective father, Fenton Hardy, in his investigations. But they also solved cases on their own—like *Cast of Criminals,* where a mystery play had turned into a real-life puzzle. Now a new mystery had fallen into their laps.

Joe slipped the letter into his pocket. "What now?"

"Well, the note says 'blow up.' Let's keep our eyes open at the Old Glory plant."

They arrived at the marina just in time to see the *Barbary Blood* come in from sailing the harbor. Joe stood on a dock, taping several minutes of the big ship's white sails glistening in the sun. Then they headed for the fireworks factory.

The factory was set on a big piece of land. The Hardys saw only building roofs over a tall sod wall topped with a wire fence. A uniformed security guard stood at the gate.

"We're from WBPT-TV." Frank leaned out of the van and handed over the invitation from the public relations department. "We're taping the Founders' Day preparations."

"This is from the publicity department," the guard said. "But I don't see a security pass.

Stay here, please." He picked up the guardhouse phone. "Mr. Lamont, I have two young men in a van here to do some taping for WBPT."

The guard winced as he listened, then hung up, shaking his head. "Well, I can let you in, but the boss isn't thrilled about it."

He handed Frank a map. "You're here, at Gate A. Follow the printed route to Building Seven. You'll see a sign for visitors' parking right by the door. Go in and tell the receptionist that Mr. Lamont is expecting you."

Frank thanked the guard and drove slowly onto the grounds. The road curved, taking them through a section about the size of a football field, with earth embankments and dugouts like caves in the raw earth. "What is this?" Frank asked.

Joe checked the map. "Explosives storage," he said.

"I thought so." Frank speeded up slightly. "You know, I didn't expect such tight security."

"Neither did I," Joe said. "We'd better be careful with this Lamont guy. Sounds like he's got a short fuse."

Frank rolled his eyes as they pulled into the visitor's parking space. "Can those jokes when we meet this guy. We don't need to give him any reason to kill our taping."

They stepped out of the van, carrying their taping equipment, and walked into the build-

ing. "Mr. Lamont is expecting us," Frank told the receptionist.

"Right." The young man behind the desk nodded. "Straight down this corridor—his office is the last door on the left."

The boys headed down the corridor, then Joe knocked on a door marked Clinton Lamont, Chief of Security.

A raspy voice called, "In!"

"*Real* friendly," Joe whispered as he opened the door.

Behind a huge desk, a big man was scowling at a piece of paper. "Have a seat," he grunted.

Frank and Joe sat on two folding chairs near the door, watching as Clinton Lamont read.

The security chief was easily two hundred pounds and over six feet tall. With his ruddy face and crew-cut white hair, he looked like a tough cop—and sounded like one. "So you're the Hardys, huh?"

"Yes, sir," Joe said quickly.

"This is a copy of the memo inviting you to come in and film," Lamont growled. "I don't know why those idiot PR people would let a couple of kids into places where they could get hurt."

"We're not exactly kids, Mr. Lamont," Frank said. "I'm—"

"What do you know about fireworks?"

Joe shrugged. "We've set off a few."

"That's all we need," Lamont said. "This

plant can be dangerous—*very* dangerous. People never seem to realize that. Even our own PR guys need reminding from time to time. We don't need untrained outsiders stumbling around here."

Frank glanced over at Joe, who was trying hard not to crack up.

"Here are the ground rules." Lamont rose from behind his desk. "You go nowhere on these grounds without me or one of my assistants. If you have questions, you ask me or one of my assistants. And to interview someone, you get—"

"You or one of your assistants," Joe chimed in.

Lamont glared at him. "You get my permission, wise guy. And, most important of all, you follow every recommended safety measure *as though your lives depended on it.*"

Lamont led the Hardys back outside, where a company pickup waited for them. He drove to a long one-story building in the middle of a field. As they went inside, Joe carried their video camera and Frank had the microphone. All three wore hard hats.

Shelves along the side walls of the building were full of brightly colored cardboard tubes. Frank recognized glaring red skyrocket bodies and candy-striped roman candles. But these were ignored by the workers, who were packing two-foot-long metal tubes—more like four-inch pipes—into wooden crates. As far as Frank and Joe could tell, no one seemed worried about any possible explosions.

"What goes on in here?" Frank asked.

"Nothing much to interest you," Lamont said. "These people are assembling some of the fireworks mortars for the Founders' Day show." Now that he mentioned it, the metal tubes did look like miniature cannons. Joe filmed them with more interest.

"Usually this is where we load gunpowder into the fireworks we sell," Lamont went on. "You can see the difference between professional fireworks and the stuff the amateurs play with." He glanced scornfully from the businesslike mortars to the gaudy merchandise that had been put aside.

The boys watched the workers load crates onto a conveyor belt, which stretched down the long room, then through an opening in a wall.

"Will we see the other end of the building?" Joe asked, shooting some footage of the moving belt.

"Yes." Lamont abruptly led the way into the other room. "We had to walk through here because there's no parking at that end. In fact, there aren't even any entrances. Only exit doors, in case a spark hits the powder."

Each side of the building was lined with a series of doors marked Emergency Exit. Between the doors, the boys saw signs that repeated two messages over and over: Absolutely No Smoking! and Danger! Explosives!

"Get a shot of that row of doors," Frank said. Joe knelt on one knee and aimed at the doors, slowly panning the camera.

"This is all for the workers' safety," Lamont said. "No one in this area is ever more than thirty feet from one of these exits. They're locked from the outside at all times, but a light push on those panic bars opens them immediately. Opening one of these doors also sets off alarms all over the plant."

Joe laughed. "If you keep them locked all the time, how can you be sure they'll work in an emergency?"

"Good question," Lamont said, giving Joe another acid look. "My people test the doors once a day, between noon and one o'clock. Of course, they turn off the alarm system during the test."

Lamont stomped off, reeling off facts and figures. Frank tried to take notes, but Lamont hardly gave him a chance. He talked—and walked—like a man who wanted very much to be somewhere else.

As Lamont rushed ahead of the Hardys, Joe stopped in his tracks, staring at the side wall. Frank glanced curiously back at his brother.

"What are you two doing?" Lamont said, annoyed. "I told you to stay with me."

"Mr. Lamont—" Joe began.

"I've had enough. If you can't follow me, we'll end this." Lamont marched them to the opposite end of the building, onto a loading dock. "Stay right here," the security chief said. "I'll get the truck." He stomped down a set of stairs.

"Mr. Lamont!" Joe called out. "Hold it!"

The edge in his voice stopped Lamont, who turned angrily. "If this is another dumb joke—"

"You should check back there," Joe said. "One of the emergency doors was open."

Lamont's face was about the color of brick. "I've had enough of your fooling around," he said. "Those doors are locked—every one of them."

"Look, I saw it!" Joe said. "Someone stuck a little piece of wood—"

"Those doors are locked!" Lamont repeated. "If one opens, the whole alarm system goes off. Do you hear any alarms?"

Frank said, "No, but—"

"Then stop talking nonsense!" Lamont turned and headed for the truck.

The Hardys watched him go. "Are you sure you saw an open door?" Frank asked.

"Lamont can yell all he wants," Joe told him. "One of those doors was *open.*"

"Well, it doesn't matter, if he's going to throw us out," Frank said.

"Right," Joe said. "So we might as well film what we can." Camera ready, he stepped through the open back of a trailer truck that stood at the loading dock. "Looks like this stuff is going to the *Barbary Blood.*"

The truck was filled with decorations and equipment for the Founders' Day celebration. Joe panned his camera, then stopped. "So, fireworks pros aren't interested in that silly kid stuff, huh? So why are *these* here?"

Frank peered through the door as Joe knelt by a cardboard box full of extra-large, bright-red firecrackers. "A box like that could make a pretty big bang," he said. "Why would the technicians need them on the *Barbary Blood?*"

"Somebody's sneaking them out of the factory for a private celebration," Joe said. He looked more closely at the box. Then he moved one of the firecrackers.

Joe's hand pulled back as if he'd just seen a snake. "There's a lit fuse in there!" he shouted. "This stuff is about to go up!"

2 Behind the Mystery Door

Joe frantically spilled the box over and snatched up the oversized firecracker, its fuse still sputtering. He tossed the explosive onto the open concrete of the loading dock. It went off with a sharp blast just as Lamont pulled up in the pickup truck.

"What was that? And what are you doing in here?" Lamont demanded, stomping into the truck.

"I was just getting a shot of the equipment for the Founders' Day show," Joe explained. "Then I found someone had rigged this box of firecrackers to explode."

"Come on. We wouldn't be using penny-ante stuff like firecrackers on the *Barbary Blood.*" But Lamont's scoffing stopped when he saw the miniature bombs scattered around.

The security man straightened, glaring suspiciously at the Hardys. "What are you two trying to pull?"

"Us?" Joe said. "Now, wait a minute!"

"No," Lamont said. "*You* wait a minute. Your fairy tale about the open door was annoying. But throwing lit firecrackers around could have gotten somebody hurt—even *killed.* Keep up this kind of nonsense, and I'll see you banned from these premises for good."

Lamont stormed back to the truck. Frank and Joe just looked at each other and silently shook their heads.

Moments later, they were driving back home. "Well, so much for spending the day taping," Frank said.

"Yeah—but we do have something to look at." As soon as they were in the house, they rushed into the living room. Frank turned on the TV. Joe took the tape cassette from his camera, slipped it into the VCR, and pressed the play button. He sped the tape up to the shot of the emergency doors.

The boys watched closely as the first door and the warning signs appeared. Then came the second door, the third, and the fourth.

Joe suddenly stabbed the freeze button as the screen showed another of the emergency doors. "Look," he said. A line of light appeared along one side of the door, and a small piece of wood had been wedged in near the bottom to keep the door open.

"Now do you believe me?" Joe said.

"I never said I didn't," Frank said. "But I'm glad we have some proof."

Joe pressed the stop button and rewound the tape. "So what do you think is going on?"

"Hard to say," Frank said. "But if Lamont is such a bug on security, how did he miss this?"

"Maybe he didn't," Joe said.

"You mean Lamont is lying?" Frank asked.

Joe nodded.

"So, the security chief knows his security is lousy and lies to reporters about it." Frank shrugged. "Maybe he's scared he'll lose his job."

"Or," Joe said, "maybe it has something to do with that note we got this morning."

"Could be," Frank said. "Where does the box of firecrackers fit in?"

"I have a theory about that," Joe said. "The rest of the stuff on that truck wasn't explosive. It would have been ruined—"

"And we'd have been scared out of our skins," Frank added with a laugh. Then he got serious. "But why? Unless somebody doesn't want us taping on the grounds."

"And we know someone who doesn't want us on the grounds," Joe went on. "Lamont."

Frank frowned. "But how could he have set up that box of fireworks? He was with us."

"That firecracker had a slow fuse," Joe said. "And we don't know how long the fuse was when it was first lit."

"And the whole thing ends with Lamont tossing us out and telling us not to come back," Frank said. "That's not a bad theory you have there, except for a couple of holes—like a real reason for Lamont not wanting us around."

Joe looked at his brother. "Any ideas on how we find it out?"

"I can think of a first step," Frank said. "Let's go talk to Con Riley."

He and Frank hurried out to their van.

Officer Con Riley was their strongest link with the Bayport police. Chief Collig wasn't happy about amateurs invading his crime-fighting turf. Riley, on the other hand, would often accept their help—and sometimes even give them a helping hand.

Frank parked the van outside the police station, and he and Joe went inside. Con Riley spotted them before they saw him. He waved to them from behind a file cabinet as he slid a drawer closed.

"Here comes trouble," Con said with a smile. "What's up, guys?"

Frank and Joe both grinned back. "Hi, Con," Joe said. "Listen, we need a little favor."

"What a surprise," Con said, leading them to his desk. "You know, the last time you paid me a friendly call, you happened to need a favor, too."

The boys took seats, and Frank ran through their problem, carefully not mentioning the note they'd received or their suspicions about Lamont.

"So, Clint Lamont tossed you out?" Con said, laughing at the end of their story.

"Well, not exactly," Joe said.

"He escorted you to the exit?" Con asked. "And he told you not to come back?"

"Sure, but—"

Con laughed again. "Okay, he didn't actually kick you through the gate, but it sounds like being thrown out to me. Where do I come in?"

"Maybe you could call him," Frank said. "Tell him we're not troublemakers. You know, soften him up a little. If we can't tape at the plant, our whole report goes down the tubes."

Con shrugged. "I know Lamont—and he owes me some. I'll give him a call and see what happens." Frank and Joe stepped away while Con made the phone call. They were looking over the Wanted posters when they heard Chief Collig's voice.

"Look, the town supervisor wants it done," Collig was saying. "I don't care who complains about it." He turned a corner and almost walked right into Frank.

"Oh, great," Collig said, "the boy detectives. Are you here to give me a hard time?"

"No, Chief," Frank said, smiling. "We're just visiting our friend Con."

"Officer Riley is too busy to be entertaining friends," Collig said, walking past the boys. "Make it a short visit."

"Right, Chief," Joe called after him.

They turned around to see Con hanging up the phone. He waved them over.

"Good news," Con said. "I got you a second chance. But it comes with a strict condition."

"What's that?" Joe asked.

"No taping without direct supervision. Lamont wants to be sure that you two 'Report the news and don't try to cause any,' was the way he put it."

"What?" Joe said.

Frank added, "We didn't do any—"

"I know," Con said. "You already told me what happened. But Lamont is convinced that somehow you were responsible for those firecrackers. So watch your step. I won't be able to help you again."

"We'll be careful," Frank said. "And thanks, Con."

"Don't mention it," Con said. "Stop in again sometime. When you don't need anything."

Back at the plant, Frank and Joe had no trouble getting past the gate guard. This time, though, Lamont didn't meet them at Building 7. Instead, they were greeted by a young man who didn't look much older than Frank.

"Hi," he said. "I'm Lew Collins, one of Mr. Lamont's assistants."

"Frank Hardy," Frank said, "and this is my brother, Joe."

Collins shook hands with both of them. As the boys climbed into his pickup truck, he said,

"Mr. Lamont said you were taping at Building Two. He wants me to take you out there again."

He drove off as Joe closed the door. "Just what are you hoping to tape?" Collins asked.

Frank smiled. "Anything that might make our feature more interesting," he said.

"You're covering the Founders' Day celebration," Collins said. "Mr. Lamont told me. Well, I won't tell you what to tape and what not to tape. Just stick close to me. Not that I could do much for you if anything went wrong in one of those buildings." Collins chuckled to show he was only joking.

In Building 2 they followed the same route Lamont had taken. But this time, the workers were gone. The conveyor belt was covered with bright tubes and gunpowder.

"Have you seen these?" Collins handed Joe a couple of dull gray lumps about the size of marbles.

"What are they?" Joe asked.

"Stars," Collins said. "They're what a rocket throws off to make those brilliant displays. They burn at about two thousand degrees."

Joe opened his hand as if the stars had burned him. "I'll shoot a picture of them while you tell us that again," he said.

After a few minutes of taping, they moved on till they reached the door the Hardys had been eagerly looking for. Neither of them was surprised to find it securely locked.

When they had gone through the whole

building, Collins led Frank and Joe out onto the loading dock. "Listen," he said, "I have to get the truck. Do you want to come with me, or would you rather wait here?"

Frank said, "We might as well come—"

"We'll wait here!" Joe cut in.

Frank looked at him, wondering what Joe was up to.

"Uh—the video equipment," Joe said quickly. "I'd rather not lug it around any more than we have to."

Frank nodded, pretending that he understood his brother's motives.

"Okay," Collins said. "Be back in about five minutes." He disappeared inside the building.

Frank gave his brother a look. "Since when can't you handle less than ten pounds of camera?"

"I needed a quick excuse." Joe pointed to the side of the building. "Look!"

Frank stared at the row of doors. Each one bore a sign that read Emergency Exit—Absolutely No Entrance!

"The third one from the right," Joe said. "That's the door that was wedged open this morning. Look at the steps coming down from it."

Joe stepped to a concrete stairway that led below ground level, to a basement door. Kneeling, he said, "I see footprints on the steps. They were made by some kind of white powder."

"And they're leading away from that door down there," Frank added.

They dashed downward, to find the door at the bottom unlocked. "Let's make this quick!" Joe said, stumbling forward into a dark, musty room. "I don't want us thrown off the grounds again."

They began searching the dim room, finding floor-to-ceiling shelves of cardboard boxes labeled with the names of fireworks. The floor was covered with a fine white powder.

"Joe!" Frank whispered. "Over here! Quick!"

Joe crossed the room to his brother, who was bent over, looking at a carton.

"It's been torn open," Frank said. "And half of what should be in there is missing."

The carton was labeled Super Torpedoes and it had a big gap in the middle. "You know, these boxes look just like the one that was in the back of the trailer truck," he said.

"We don't have any more time," Joe said. "Lew will be back any second."

They headed back toward the door. As Joe reached to push it open, they heard a chilling sound.

"I just took a look at this door!" Lamont's voice boomed, directly above them. "I want it fixed, and I want it fixed now."

He was so close that he might have been screaming at Joe and Frank. They quietly eased away from the door and back into the room.

"The wires have been cut on this door," they heard Lamont say. "The emergency exits are all wired into the alarms. Cut the wires, and this door is useless as a security device."

Lamont fell silent, as though listening to the unlucky person on the other end of this conversation.

"What do we do now?" Joe whispered.

"Hope real hard that Lamont doesn't decide to come down here."

As Frank answered, he heard heavy footsteps on the stairs outside. Grabbing Joe's arm, he pulled him behind some cartons just as the door jerked open.

Frank peered through a crack in the pile of cartons.

Lamont barked "Goodbye!" into the portable phone in his hand, rammed the antenna down, and jammed the phone into his jacket pocket.

He pulled out a flashlight, aiming it into the corners of the room. Frank and Joe held their breath as the beam swept toward them.

3 Out of the Dark

Joe and Frank crouched frozen behind the cartons as the light came closer. Then it stopped. A muffled, twittering sound reached the Hardys' ears.

The security chief pulled the phone from his pocket again. "Lamont here," he said. Then, listening for a second, he took a long, fuming breath. "Those papers are in my office. Hold on a minute."

The boys stayed motionless as Lamont stomped up the stairs. Then Frank stepped from behind the cartons. "He's gone. Let's hope Collins isn't back with that truck."

The boys ran to the top of the stairs just as the pickup truck turned the corner.

Moments later, as they climbed aboard the pickup, Collins said, "I hope you got what you came for today."

"We have some good footage," Frank said. "But we'll need at least one more trip out here.

I'd like to see that assembly line in production, and maybe see the explosives storage area. And it would be nice to see the preparations on the *Barbary Blood. . . .*"

"That's a pretty tall order," Collins said as he drove the Hardys to their van. "You might be able to see the assembly line, but I don't know about the explosives. And Mr. Lamont is trying to keep everybody away from that boat."

Collins shrugged. "I'll do what I can. In the meantime, don't hesitate to call me if you need information." He smiled. "You know, statistics, or facts about fireworks, stuff like that. I usually work nights—overtime for this big hoedown."

"Great," Joe said as he and Frank loaded their equipment into the van.

"Thanks again," Frank called as Collins drove away. He got into the van and started it up.

"Well," Joe said, "what now?"

Frank thought for a moment. "I think we should see Con Riley again," he said. "He seems to know Lamont. If he gives us the story on Lamont's background, maybe we can figure out what makes Lamont so nervous about having people around the factory and the boat."

They pulled into the police-station parking lot just as Con Riley was walking toward his own car.

"Hey, Con!" Joe called. "Could you tell us—"

"Lamont's an ex-cop," Con said, cutting him

off. "He was on the force for twenty years, over in Twelve Pines."

Joe blinked. "How did you know—"

Con just shook his head. "I have a sixth sense about Hardys. You guys are never satisfied with just one visit. Something else always comes to you just after you visit me."

"What else can you tell us about him?" Joe asked.

"There really isn't all that much to tell," Con said, flipping open a notepad. "He walked a beat for about ten years. Then he got a promotion to desk sergeant. He has one commendation, for outstanding attendance. Over a certain five-year period, he didn't take a single sick day."

"Anything else?" Frank asked.

"Not much," Con said. "He ran the auxiliary police force for two years, just before he retired. As soon as he was off the force, he got the job at Old Glory. That was eight years ago."

The boys thanked Con and he got into his car and drove away.

"Lamont had a solid career," Frank said to Joe. "But you couldn't call it outstanding."

"Maybe the guy just works hard and gets jittery about having anyone around the plant. He could just be afraid for his job." Joe shook his head. "The question is, where do we go from here?"

"We go home," Frank said. "Phil Cohen's coming over after dinner to talk about the lights we'll need to tape the celebration. Remember, we still have a job to do."

"So you've hired an outside genius to help me?" Joe asked with a grin. Phil was a good friend, who could also do incredible things with electronics. If Phil were taking care of the lights, Joe's job would be a lot easier.

"By the way, Frank," Joe went on, "I've been thinking about that note. You know I don't like to jump to conclusions . . ."

Frank hid a smile. If jumping to conclusions were an Olympic event, Joe would have a closet full of gold medals.

"But sometimes a hunch gets so strong that you just can't ignore it." Joe looked at his brother. "I think the person who wrote the note was trying to warn us about Lamont."

"I've heard crazier notions," Frank said.

Joe smiled. "That's a relief. I thought you'd tell me I was acting without evidence."

"Well, of course you are," Frank said. "All we know about Lamont is that he doesn't want us around that fireworks factory. Anyone could have planted that burning firecracker. But Lamont is the only one who knew we'd be out there right then. So I'm not laughing at your hunch."

"What should we do about it?" Joe asked.

"I'm not sure," Frank said. "Lamont's got us blocked."

"Maybe not. How about paying a visit to the place when Lamont isn't around?"

"That could be risky," Frank said. "How would we get in?"

"I've already thought of that," Joe said. "We just say we need a night shot of the outside of the plant for contrast."

Frank nodded.

"Why not head over there tonight? We'll bring Phil with us, so he can set up some lights as a test. If we're lucky, we might be able to uncover something while Lamont is home in bed."

A slow smile came over Frank's face. "Fine. We'll do it after dinner."

At eight on the dot, Phil Cohen's lanky frame appeared in the Hardys' doorway. "Hello, Phil," Mrs. Hardy said. "Come on in."

"Hi, Mrs. Hardy." Phil ran a hand through his dark hair. "Are the guys—"

"Ready—yup," Joe said, coming down the stairs with Frank. "How's it going, Phil?"

"Not bad," Phil answered. "I have all the lights in the car."

"Good," Joe said. "Let's move them into the van. We're going out to Old Glory to do some night shooting."

"Now?" Phil didn't look happy.

"That's right," Joe said, leading the way out of the house. "It'll be a great test, don't you think?"

Minutes later, Frank pulled the van up to the guard's post at the Old Glory factory entrance. "Hi," he said, handing the guard his pass.

"Frank and Joe Hardy, from WBPT-TV. And Phil Cohen, our lighting assistant."

In the back of the van, Phil snorted.

The guard looked at the pass, picked up his phone, and punched in three numbers. After a few seconds, he said, "Mr. Collins? I've got a couple of guys from WBPT."

He hung up the phone and motioned in the direction of the main building. Frank drove onto the grounds.

"Okay, Phil," Frank said. "After we park, we'll set up those two arc lamps and train them on the front of the main building."

"Right," Phil said.

As soon as Frank parked, he and Joe hopped out of the van to help Phil unload. Lew Collins appeared in the doorway. "Evening, guys," he said.

"Hi, Lew," Frank said. "This is Phil Cohen, a friend of ours. He's also our resident lighting expert. Phil, meet Lew Collins."

Phil shook hands. "Pleased to meet you."

"Likewise," Collins said. "What are you guys doing here so late? Looking to capture the mystery of a fireworks plant at night?"

"Not exactly," Joe said. "We just thought we'd like to open with a quiet night shot for contrast, since we're closing with the explosive night of the show."

The sounds of the crickets were joined by a series of electronic beeps.

"That's me." Collins pushed a button on the

pager clipped to his belt. "I have to return this call. You guys can get along on your own for a while, can't you?"

"Sure thing," Frank said. "We'll be right here."

As Collins walked away, Joe began scanning the grounds. Phil plugged one of the lights into the mobile generator in the back of the van. He switched the light on and walked to the front of the van to work on another one.

A bright glare lit up part of the building front that had been pitch-black. Frank and Joe found themselves staring at a man who stood in the circle of light, shielding his eyes.

The man stepped closer to them. He was of medium height and athletically built, with brown curly hair. He wore a sports jacket and a bright printed tie.

Still shielding his eyes, he said, "You're the crew from the TV station, aren't you?"

"You got it—but right now we're more interested in what *you're* doing out here."

The man stepped out from the glare of the light. "That's some powerful light you have there. Too bad you didn't have it on before I came out. I heard noises and went to investigate." He smiled and held out his hand. "I'm Don Munder. I work in research and development here at Old Glory."

The Hardys introduced themselves and Phil. As he shook hands, Munder's eyes kept darting around, as though he were looking for something. Or maybe watching out for something.

"Is anything wrong?" Joe asked. He switched off the light, which seemed to make Munder relax.

"Wrong?" Munder smiled pleasantly, shaking his head. But he continued to look around, past the boys. "I just thought I'd ask if there's anything my department might contribute to the feature you're taping."

Joe glanced sharply at the man. "Thanks," he said, "but we'll have to check in with Mr. Lamont, who's supervising our visits here."

"We only have about seven minutes, including about two minutes of the fireworks show itself," Frank explained. "So we probably won't even have time for extra material." He looked to see if Joe would help him fish for information.

Joe did. "Unless we wind up with a story that's more than we can cover in a seven-minute feature."

"What do you mean?" Munder asked.

"There's been a rumor about possible trouble at the celebration." That sounds vague enough, Frank thought.

"Trouble?" Munder's voice grew sharp. "What kind of trouble?"

Frank decided to try a shot in the dark. "What would you say if we told you that someone was out to sabotage the Founders' Day fireworks show?"

Munder licked his lips nervously. He was about to answer when he looked over the Hardys' shoulders. His face paled.

"I'd say that was nonsense," said a voice from the darkness. All heads turned in that direction. "Sabotage, huh?" Frank and Joe had no doubt whose voice it was.

Clinton Lamont stepped out of the darkness. Behind him, the Hardys saw the outline of another man. As he stepped closer, they saw that the man's right arm was missing.

Frank noticed how Munder tightened up when he spotted Lamont. Lamont was busy glaring at the Hardys.

"Why, Mr. Lamont—what a surprise." At least Joe was being honest.

Lamont scowled. "I thought I said that you two were not to be on any part of these grounds unsupervised."

"Well, sir," Frank said, "we *were* being supervised. But Mr. Collins had to go inside to answer a phone—"

"I'm not interested." Lamont cut him off. "Now, what's this garbage about sabotage?"

Frank and Joe glanced at each other. Should they tell about the note they'd gotten? "We can't reveal our source, Mr. Lamont," Joe said.

"Oh, of course not," Lamont said. "But you can pull the worst junk-journalism tricks to try and make up an exciting story for yourselves."

He thrust his face into Joe's. "Look, kid, I'm responsible for security around here. And that includes most parts of the Founders' Day celebration. So, when you talk about a security problem, you're smearing my reputation."

"Mr. Lamont," Joe said, "we didn't mean—"

"I don't care what you meant," Lamont said. "I don't need people who can't tell the difference between reporting news and inventing stories that hurt people."

Then Lamont turned to Don Munder. "And just what are you doing here with these two?"

"He was just asking about our equipment," Joe said quickly.

Lamont and Munder stared at each other, ignoring Joe. Each looked as though he'd like to rearrange the features of the other man's face.

Then the security man broke the silence. "These boys are leaving the premises. If you're so interested in their equipment, Mr. Munder, perhaps you'd like to accompany them off the grounds."

"I was actually heading home," Munder said. "Sorry I can't take care of your errand."

Lamont glared at him. "You're not playing with fireworks now, Munder. You're playing with dynamite—and people can get hurt that way."

Phil, Frank, and Joe hurriedly loaded their gear into the van. They all climbed in, and Frank started the engine.

Lamont appeared at the driver's window.

"You'll return to these premises only—and I stress *only* —if and when I give you permission. Until then, I don't want to see you, your brother, or that clown with the lights. Good night!"

Frank turned the van around and drove past the guardhouse. The three boys were silent until they were well off the grounds.

"Lamont seemed as angry with Munder as he was with us," Joe said.

Frank nodded. "That's because Munder was about to tell us something. I'd like to ask Mr. M. about that."

"Can I make a suggestion?" Phil asked.

Both brothers turned to him.

"If you're going to meet this Munder guy, meet him on the other side of town." Phil frowned as he spoke. "I was looking at Lamont's face back there when he told Munder he was playing with dynamite—and could get hurt."

A shudder went up Phil's thin shoulders. "I think Lamont meant every word he said. And he might not mind who else gets hurt, either."

4 More Rumors of Sabotage

The next morning, Frank dialed the number for the Old Glory factory and asked for Don Munder. "Hello, Mr. Munder?" he said into the telephone. "Frank Hardy. My brother and I were thinking about your offer to help us last night. I wonder if we could get together."

Joe watched while Frank switched the phone to his other hand, writing something down. "Good," Frank said. "We'll see you in an hour."

"Where do we see him?" Joe asked as Frank hung up.

"A restaurant called Abe and Mabel's," Frank said. "It's across town, near Willow Street and the river."

"I guess he's going there for lunch," Joe said. "I wonder what kind of place Abe and Mabel's is."

Joe began to get an idea as he and Frank headed west and south, out past the residential part of town and into an industrial park.

"Forget the what—*why* Abe and Mabel's?" Joe wondered aloud.

"I don't have a clue," Frank said. "Maybe he wants us as far from the plant as possible. You saw the way Lamont talked to him."

Two miles later, Frank turned the van onto a street lined with factories and warehouses. Then he came to an auto graveyard, with a pile of junked cars spilling over onto the parking lot next door. In the middle of the lot was a diner—Abe and Mabel's.

Frank rolled the van into the gravel parking lot and stopped. The lot was almost empty.

"Wow, Munder sure has classy taste," Joe groused, gazing at the run-down restaurant.

Frank shrugged. "We'll go inside and wait."

The restaurant was a stucco building badly in need of a paint job. The gravel near the building was white with stucco chips that had flaked off.

A bare bulb lit up a sign that said Abe and M bel's. The missing *A* had probably disappeared years ago.

Frank reached for the screen door, then jumped back as a cat ran in front of him. When he pulled the door open, a loud squeak welcomed them into the diner.

One look showed that Munder wasn't there

yet. Frank and Joe sat in a booth and ordered. The waiter brought their sodas, and shortly afterward, the door creaked open again. The boys turned to see Don Munder walk in.

He spotted them and headed over. On the way, he ordered a cup of coffee.

"Sorry I'm late," Munder said. "I lost track of time. What did you want to talk to me about?"

"For starters," Joe said, "what's the real danger of accidents during one of these shows? Lamont acts as if everything out there can blow up."

Munder shook his head. "Lamont got spooked by a near-accident we had last year. A fire broke out in one of the assembly-line buildings. It was put out before it reached anything explosive. Even if it had—well, that's why the buildings at the plant are spread out so much."

"But is there a danger?" Joe asked.

"Most of the excitement over the fire was in the press." Munder shrugged. "Sure, there's some danger. There always is when explosives are involved. But you have a better chance of getting hurt on your drive home than you would at a fireworks show."

"Does that chance worry the company enough to put heavy security around the preparations?" Frank asked.

"How do you mean?"

"Well," Frank said, "I see how gung ho Lamont is acting. Could it be because someone wants to mess up the show—"

"Oh, that 'sabotage' thing you mentioned last night," Munder said. "Well, Lamont *has* been acting like more of an idiot lately. But I think that's more because the big boss is out of town, negotiating for another show. Lamont doesn't want anything going wrong while Mr. Samms is away."

"What *could* go wrong?" Joe asked.

The waiter brought Munder's coffee. He took a sip before answering Joe's question.

"I suppose almost anything. The fireworks mortars use real artillery shells to throw the rockets into the air. If the shells blew up, they could sink the *Barbary Blood.*" He shuddered. "And there's enough explosive material at the factory to take Bayport off the map. But tampering with any of that would have to be an inside job. I mean, Lamont himself would be the best suspect. With his job, he knows all the security precautions. But, of course, he wouldn't be interested."

"Who *would* want to sabotage the show?" Frank asked.

Munder shrugged. "I couldn't say. Unless it was Northern Lights—the Northern Lights Fireworks Company, up in Massachusetts. They're Old Glory's most serious competition. Every year they bid for the Founders' Day show, but naturally it goes to the home team. I know people over at Northern Lights who might bend rules to get that contract—it means big money." He shook his head. "But sabotage? No, I can't believe it."

He took another sip of coffee. "But if you boys want to punch up your feature, I have a terrific suggestion."

"What's that?" Frank asked.

"Why not talk with some old-time employees from Old Glory—get reminiscences of former celebrations?"

"We've already included that in our plan," Joe said.

"Good," Munder said. "But you may want to go a step further. How about getting in touch with former employees—people who retired or left the company for other reasons?"

"That's something we never thought about," Frank said.

Munder finished his coffee. "Tell you what. I'll get you a list of former employees."

"A list?" Joe said, surprised.

"The company keeps a file on all former employees," Munder said. "Anybody who leaves the company goes into that file."

"What for?" Joe asked.

Munder frowned. "If you asked, they'd come up with a dozen reasonable excuses. But the real reason is that Clinton Lamont is a suspicious fool."

His voice slowly rose, until the last phrase came out louder than he expected. Embarrassed, Munder lowered his voice. "Look, a lot of things that go on in an explosives plant are very hush-hush. If Old Glory develops a new kind of firework, they don't want some unhappy employee taking it to one of their competitors."

Joe said, "So they keep a file—"

"To keep track of where everybody is," Munder said.

"Could you get us this file?" Joe asked.

Munder slowly smiled. "It's not secret—and I wouldn't mind putting one over on Lamont. But I wouldn't want people knowing that *I* gave it out."

"Who's going to tell?" Frank asked.

"Okay—I'll photocopy it as soon as I go back to work," Munder said. "I'll have it for you tonight."

"Terrific," Joe said. "Where can we meet you? We can drive to the plant, if you like."

"Oh, no," Munder said. "Too close to Lamont. Why don't I meet you in front of the post office. Say, eight o'clock?"

"We'll be there," Joe said.

"See you then." Munder stood, dropped a dollar on the table, and headed out.

Frank and Joe waited until they heard Munder's car pull away. Then they left.

"Frank," Joe said, "what are we going to do with this file? We'll wind up with enough good-old-days stories to fill a three-hour broadcast."

"We're not looking for stories," Frank said. "I'm hoping we'll get some hard facts about Old Glory. That file's full of people who don't have to worry what they say about the company." He frowned. "Besides, if there's any truth behind that note we got, an angry ex-employee could be the person we're looking for."

After dinner, Frank and Joe drove downtown, parking in front of the post office. Munder was already there, sitting in a car across the street. He got out and walked over to their van.

"Here you go," Munder said, holding out a thick manila envelope.

"Thanks, Mr. Munder." Frank took the file from him. "I'm sure we'll put this to good use."

Munder smiled, waved, and went back to his car. The boys watched him drive off.

Frank handed the file to Joe and pulled away from the post office. Then he drove to the Liberty Bell Diner in the center of town. They went inside, straight to their favorite booth. Their girlfriends, Callie Shaw and Iola Morton, were waiting for them.

"Hi, guys," Callie said, her dark eyes shining.

"Hey, Callie," Joe said, smiling. He sat next to Iola.

Frank sat next to Callie. He said, "How are the plans going for your Founders' Day float?"

"Pretty good," Iola said, her pixie face lighting up in a grin. "We've already finished the wire model for it."

"Tomorrow," Callie said, "we have to pick up the azalea wreath to decorate it. I think this is going to be the best Founders' Day yet."

"I don't know how we could top last year's parade," Iola said. "Chet held up the whole line of march when he pulled over on Main Street and tried to get a hot dog from one of the street vendors. The entire town saw that stunt."

Joe and Frank looked at each other. "There may be a worse one this year," Frank said. "Somebody sent us a note threatening the fireworks display."

"We're going to talk to a few people about it tomorrow." Joe grinned. "We don't want anyone raining on those azaleas—or on the rest of the parade."

The next morning, when Frank came down for breakfast, Joe was talking on the phone.

"Yes," Joe said. "I see. All right, Mr. Gallagher. Thank you."

When Joe hung up, Frank said, "Who was that?"

"Michael Gallagher," Joe said. "A former maintenance worker at Old Glory. He has nothing but good things to say about Lamont, Munder, and the whole gang down at Old Glory."

"Was that your first call?" Frank asked, buttering a piece of toast.

"Nope," Joe said, looking through the file folder. "I'm already up to G. Norman Gaines, who used to work there as a guard, now lives in a retirement community in Tucson, Arizona."

Frank turned the file so they could both see the list of names. "What about Fran Galvin?" he asked.

"Deceased," Joe said.

"Corinne Guster?"

"She married another former employee, a guy named Edward Belson. He happens to be an ex-Green Beret with special training in explosives."

Frank leaned forward. "Now we're getting somewhere."

"More like nowhere," Joe said. "Mr. and Mrs. Belson are now religious missionaries, working somewhere in South America."

"Next up," Frank said, scanning the list. "Anna Siegel."

Joe picked up the receiver and dialed a number. After a few seconds, he said, "Hello, Ms. Siegel? This is Joseph Hardy, from WBPT-TV. I'm trying to contact former employees of the Old Glory Fireworks Company for a segment on the Founders' Day celebration this Saturday."

He stopped talking and scrawled something on the pad he had in front of him. Then he said, "Thank you, Ms. Siegel," and hung up.

"What did she say?" Frank asked, clearing his breakfast dishes away.

"She wants to meet with us," Joe said. "She was thrilled to get the call. She wants to discuss 'some of the weird stuff' that went on at Old Glory. And she didn't want to talk about it on the phone."

"That sounds promising," Frank said. "Where and when do we meet her?"

"In front of the video store at the Bayport Mall," Joe said. "In an hour."

"Let's go now," Frank said. "We can hang out at the mall." He put on his jacket and tossed Joe's jacket to him.

Joe headed out. But just as Frank got to the door, the phone rang. He turned back and picked up the receiver. "Hello?"

"Frank Hardy?" a whispered voice on the other end said. "Get your brother Joe to the phone."

"Who are you—" Frank began, but the whispered voice cut him off.

"You still don't know the danger of playing with dynamite."

Frank whirled, staring out the kitchen window. Joe was crouched down in the driveway, looking at something under the van. He started pulling something out—it looked like a metal box.

The phone fell from Frank's hand as he leapt to the door. "Get away from that thing!" he yelled. "I think it's a bomb!"

5 A Talk with Anna Siegel

Joe didn't hesitate—as soon as Frank yelled, he threw the metal box into the backyard.

And just in time, too. A loud hissing came from the box, and Joe hit the deck. The box didn't explode, though. It just sat on the grass, seeming to sag inward on itself.

The Hardys gave it another minute or so, then cautiously approached the box. Joe reached toward it, but Frank grabbed his arm. "Don't—it's still too hot."

Frank edged the box over with the toe of his hiking boot to reveal scorched grass underneath.

Joe stared. "What was *in* that thing?"

"I'd say we just saw a homemade thermite grenade." Frank's face was grim. "Two thousand degrees would be needed to melt this down."

"Two thousand degrees?" Joe echoed. "I'm glad I got it out of my hands in time." He stared at the sagging box with a lot more respect. "You think it was homemade?"

"Oh, anybody with a good chemistry lab could have made it," Frank said. "Or access to fireworks materials."

Joe gave him a look. "A lot of work—just to play a prank on us."

"I hope it was just a prank," Frank said, heading back to the van to check it over carefully. "All that heat was supposed to be let off under our gas tank."

Silently, Joe joined him in searching the van.

Because of the search, they got to the mall ten minutes later than they'd agreed to meet Anna Siegel. They jumped out of the van and ran to the entrance at top speed.

Vinnie's Video was right in the middle of the mall, so the boys had to struggle with some crowds to reach it. When they got to the store, they skidded to a halt.

"I hope we didn't miss her," Joe said, looking around.

They both scanned the area, looking for a woman who might be Anna Siegel. Then a short woman in sunglasses and a gray coat stepped up in front of Frank.

"Mr. Hardy?" she asked.

"Yes, ma'am. I'm Frank Hardy."

"Oh," she said. "I was looking for a Joseph Hardy."

Joe stepped forward and smiled. "I'm Joe Hardy," he said. "My brother and I are both reporting on the Founders' Day celebration."

Siegel looked at her watch. "I only have thirty minutes, or I'll be late for work," she said. "But I really did want to talk to you about Old Glory—and Clinton Lamont."

"We can talk in there," Joe said, pointing to a coffee shop.

"No," Siegel said. "If you don't mind, I'd rather stay out here. Those places are so cramped and musty."

"Whatever you say," Frank said, rolling his eyes at Joe.

The Hardys followed Anna Siegel to a row of stone benches that faced an open area. She sat in the center of a long bench, and the boys sat on either side of her.

"I was a bookkeeper at Old Glory for fourteen years," she said.

"Yes," Joe said. "The file said you quit only two months ago. Would you mind telling us why?"

"I didn't resign. I was forced to leave—and it's all because of Clinton Lamont." Anna Siegel's voice was hard and bitter. "I found a file in our copying room. It turned out to be the security plans for the Founders' Day celebration. Apparently, someone in Lamont's organization had lost it, but he accused *me* of stealing it. My job wasn't worth anything when he started after me. It took me six weeks to find work again—and it's just a part-time job at a small office."

Frank's eyes narrowed. Anna Siegel certainly had a grudge against Old Glory. As he tried to come up with a reporterlike question, she said, "But I suppose you're just doing a puff piece on the company, about the wonderful show they'll do."

"Actually, ma'am, we'd love to do some investigative reporting instead of a human-interest story," Joe said quickly. "That is, if there's anything to investigate."

"Look into Clinton Lamont," Anna Siegel said. "I have a feeling he is involved with some, let us say, shady characters."

Frank and Joe looked at each other. "What sort of characters?" Frank asked.

The woman took out a package of hard candy from her purse. "Can I offer you a candy?" she said.

"No, thanks," Joe said. "Ms. Siegel, who are these shady characters?"

"For one," she said, "there's a man named Kevin Bailey." She got up and strolled toward a display of paintings in the center of the mall. The Hardys followed her.

"Bailey is in our file of former employees," Joe said.

"He works for a competing company now," Siegel said. "It's called Northern Lights."

She stopped to look at one of the paintings. At the mention of Northern Lights, Joe and Frank exchanged a surprised look behind her back.

"I used to work late a few nights a month," Siegel said. "I was responsible for the payroll, and twice a month I had to put in some overtime. One night, about three months ago, I was working late. It was after nine o'clock, and Lamont was still in his office. Bailey came in to see him. The two of them talked for over an hour."

Frank and Joe waited for more, but she had apparently decided to stop talking.

"Is that it?" Frank said. "I'm afraid that doesn't sound very shady to me, Ms. Siegel."

"Yes, but you see, Mr. Hardy, Kevin Bailey didn't work for Old Glory at the time. He had already moved on to Northern Lights."

"And what do you make of that, Ms. Siegel?" Joe asked.

"Conspiracy," she said.

"Excuse me?" Joe said.

"I said conspiracy, Mr. Hardy. Executives at Old Glory do not socialize with executives at Northern Lights. The two companies have been locked in a fierce competition for years now. One of their biggest battles has revolved around the show that you two are working on."

As she talked, Frank's eyes lit up. He suddenly had an idea. "Ms. Siegel," he said, "can you tell us what Kevin Bailey looks like?"

She thought for a moment. "Well," she said, "he's about the same height as your brother here. He has light brown hair. And when I knew him, he had these long sideburns. Oh, and a bit of a potbelly, I suppose."

"Anything else?" Joe asked.

"Well, of course there's the evidence of his unfortunate accident," Siegel said. "The poor man lost an arm. He always used to call it his combat wound."

"Was he in combat?" Frank asked.

"No," Siegel said. "He was hurt in an auto accident. It happened several years ago."

"We saw that man at the plant the other night," Joe said.

Siegel looked surprised. "You saw Kevin Bailey at Old Glory? I'll bet he was with Lamont, wasn't he?"

"Yes, he was," Frank said.

"Did you talk with him?" she asked.

"No," Frank said. "Mr. Lamont did all the talking that night."

"Well," she said, "if you have any dealings with Bailey, be very careful."

"Why?" Joe asked.

"He's a violent man," she said. "In fact, he was fired from Old Glory for fighting."

"With another employee?" Frank asked.

"Over the years," she said, "with several employees. The man just couldn't seem to keep himself out of scuffles with people. Finally, the company decided he was too much of a risk.

They didn't want anyone with a violent personality working around their explosives."

She stood up and looked at her watch. "I'm sorry, gentlemen," she said, "but I really have to be going."

"Ms. Siegel," Frank said, "can we call you if we need more information?"

"I'd rather you didn't," Siegel said. "I don't know that I can tell you anything more than I already have. And I have to admit that I don't enjoy talking about Old Glory. I'd prefer to forget the place. Good day, gentlemen."

Anna Siegel walked away. Joe tried to stop her, but Frank grabbed his arm and pulled him back.

"Let her go," Frank said. "She's not going to say any more."

They both stood in silence. Then Joe said, "What do you think, Frank?"

"I think we should look a little further into how Ms. Siegel wound up with that file."

They began walking toward the exit. "What do you think we'll find?" Joe asked.

"I don't know," Frank said. "But she seemed a bit too eager to finger this Bailey guy. You know, *she* doesn't sound as though she's in love with Old Glory. On top of that, she seems to have it in for Lamont. No, I don't think we can just take what she says at face value."

They left the mall and headed for the van.

"How about Munder?" Joe said.

"What about him?"

"Why don't we call and ask him about Ms. Siegel? He's been pretty helpful so far. Maybe he'll give us the lowdown on her."

"Sounds like a good idea," Frank said as they both got into the van. "Now let's see if we can catch up with Phil Cohen. I'd like to hear what he can tell us about that gift you found on the driveway."

They found Phil in his house. As soon as he heard about the bomb, he got into the van. At the Hardys' house, he took a long look at the now-cooled box and the scorched patch of grass.

Phil tugged at the top of the box. "It's fused shut," he said. "You have a chisel or something we can use to cut this open?"

Frank came out with a toolbox, and Phil cut and pried the metal top away. "I think you got it right," he told Frank. "It looks as if thermite went off inside here, melting the box into one piece. Just like the thermite grenades the army uses to melt enemy machinery together."

At last the top came off to reveal a fused, glassy mess inside. "I'm afraid there's not much to say about this," Phil said. "Everything melted." He pointed to one section. "This was the detonator. You can see what's left of the wires and the radio receiver. Thermite needs a special primer. It won't go off until it's kindled by a flame of about two thousand degrees."

"That's a familiar number," Joe said.

"Didn't Lew Collins say the fireworks stars burn that hot?"

Before Frank could answer, the telephone began ringing inside the house. He headed for the kitchen.

A whispered voice greeted him as soon as he picked up the phone. "You should have thrown that bomb away instead of standing out there examining it. Aren't you getting the message? You're playing with dynamite!"

6 Not Just Scare Tactics

Frank stood for a moment as the phone at the other end was slammed down in his ear. Then he hung up and headed back out to Joe and Phil.

"Could that thing have any more surprises in it?" Frank asked Phil.

"No way. This is a burnt-out box," Phil said.

"Then let's take it inside. It seems that someone may have been watching us out here."

They headed into the house, where Frank told them about the phone call he'd just gotten. Joe moved from window to window, checking the area for anyone who might be watching the house. "Nobody's out there now," he said. "Maybe this guy just passed by."

"I'm more interested in what the guy said," Phil spoke up.

"You mean the way he ended each phone

call?" Frank said. "We *have* heard that phrase before."

Joe turned from the window. "You're right. That's what Lamont told us when he threw us out of the Old Glory factory." He frowned. "All the same, I don't think we should rule out our new friend Anna Siegel."

Frank went into the kitchen, pulled three colas from the refrigerator, popped them open, and handed one each to Phil and Joe. Then Phil and Joe sat at the kitchen table while Frank called Munder on the phone.

"Hello, Mr. Munder," Frank said. "Frank Hardy. Well, yes, we did want . . . Yes. Listen, we met with Anna Siegel today, and we wanted to talk to you about her. Sure, Abe and Mabel's is fine. See you then."

He hung up the phone and joined Joe and Phil at the table. "Three o'clock," he said. "Did you hear? I hardly had a chance to ask for a meeting. He seemed as anxious to see us as we are to see him."

At two-thirty, Frank and Joe got in their van and drove out to Abe and Mabel's. Once again, theirs was almost the only car in the parking area. And once again, they heard the squeaking door slam shut behind them. They sat at the table they had recently shared with Munder.

Less than five minutes later, Munder came in. The door slammed behind him. He looked around, nodded at the Hardys, and walked over. As he passed the counter, he ordered a cup of coffee. After he'd been served, he came over to sit at the table with Frank and Joe.

"Hello, Mr. Munder," Frank said. "Listen, thanks for meeting with us again."

"We have to make this fast," Munder said. "I don't want to be missed around the office."

"We're curious about Anna Siegel," Joe said.

"Lamont got her fired," Munder said. He took a sip of his coffee.

"On that list of ex-employees," Joe said, "it says she quit."

"I know what the file says," Munder said.

"Why was she fired?" Frank asked.

"Lamont claimed she was snooping around the plant," Munder said. "Then, late one evening, he caught her in the copying room with the security file for the Founders' Day celebration. She said she'd just found it. He said she was about to copy it. They had a big fight about it—just about the whole company wound up taking sides. But in the end, the president listened to Lamont. Anna Siegel had to go."

Munder shook his head. "Everyone thought she was a nice old lady. But she sure didn't sound like one when she cleaned out her desk—yelling that she'd make Lamont pay for firing her, that kind of thing."

Frank said, "You say he 'claimed' she was snooping around. Does that mean you don't believe it?"

Munder hesitated for a second. "It's not for me to say." He shrugged. "People do sometimes forget things in the copying room."

He reached inside his jacket pocket and took out a sheet of paper, neatly folded down the middle. "Like this, for example. It's a copy of Anna Siegel's personnel record," he said, handing it to Frank. "This may give you some information about her that you don't have yet."

Then he stood up. "I'd better get back," he said. He dropped a dollar on the table, turned, and walked quickly out the door.

Frank studied the personnel record. Joe looked out the window and watched as Munder drove away.

"Anything interesting?" he asked his brother.

"Part of this is a statement from Anna Siegel herself," Frank said. He read from the paper:

> I deny committing any wrongful acts while in the employ of Old Glory Fireworks Company. The years I've spent at Old Glory have been among the happiest of my life. While I may be leaving under questionable circumstances, I insist that I am innocent of any wrongdoing.

Frank held the paper so they could both read it. "Look at that," Joe said, pointing to the bottom of the page.

"What?"

"Down here," Joe said. "She signed an agreement that in return for special severance pay, she wouldn't sue the company.

"Maybe she needed money to keep going while she looked for another job," Frank said. "A lot of companies make deals like that nowadays."

"Yeah," Joe said, unconvinced. "She went to the trouble of writing that statement to keep her name clear. But she didn't do the one thing that might have cleared her officially."

Joe stood up and dropped some bills on the table. "I know who might be able to help us out on this point," he said.

"Who?" Frank asked.

"Lamont."

"Well, sure," Frank said, as they headed for the door. "But we aren't exactly on a buddy-buddy basis with him."

"Let me see if I can do something about that," Joe said.

"What are you talking about? The guy hates the sight of us."

"Maybe not," Joe said. "Sure, we've driven him over the edge once or twice. But he hasn't seen our good side yet. We haven't bothered him for a few days. I'll bet we can get in to see him, if we approach him in the right way." He grinned. "Flattery will get you anywhere."

"Yeah? Well, you try it," Frank said. "I'll listen from the sidelines."

An hour later, Joe had Lamont on the phone.

"Hello, Mr. Lamont," he said. "This is Joe Hardy. Right, the blond one. My brother and I were wondering if we could set up a meeting with you in your office. No, we won't be videotaping. We'd just like to talk to you. Yes, tomorrow at eleven is fine. Thank you."

"That sounded pretty easy," Frank said.

"It was," Joe said. "He surrendered without a fight. But I must admit he didn't sound any friendlier than he did the other night."

The next morning after breakfast, Frank and Joe prepared for their meeting. "Remember," Frank said, "Lamont doesn't like us, even if he was pleasant on the phone last night. So mind your manners."

"Don't worry, big brother. I will not speak unless spoken to."

"That'll be the day," Frank said.

At the entrance to the plant, Frank slowed down, but the guard waved them past. "See? *He's* warmed up to us," Joe said.

"I wouldn't go that far," Frank said. "He should recognize our van by now. And Lamont probably told him to send us right in."

Joe pulled up next to the main building. He and Frank got out, entered the building, and walked down the long hall to Lamont's office. Frank knocked.

"In!" Lamont called from inside.

Joe opened the door, and they both stepped inside.

"Ah," Lamont said. "Mr. Hardy and Mr.

Hardy. I hope you're not here to pull another dumb stunt."

"Mr. Lamont," Joe said, "you're the one—"

"We're not here to make problems," Frank said quickly. "We just want to talk to you about your plans for the Founders' Day celebration."

"Right," Joe said, picking up his cue. "Con Riley was telling us about what a fine police officer you were—how professional. We thought it might be a good idea to tell folks how you plan to make this a safer celebration."

Of course, Lamont was happy to talk about his job, and bored them for several minutes with his plans to keep the townspeople away from the *Barbary Blood,* and indeed, out of Barmet Bay while the fireworks went off. "We don't want any used rocket casings to come down on the folks watching the show," he said.

"You must be doing a lot of planning," Joe said. "Is your security file really thick?"

"How do you know about the security file?" Lamont asked suspiciously.

"An ex-employee mentioned it," Joe said. "Anna Siegel."

Lamont's face tightened into a scowl, a little heavier than his normal scowl. "Oh, our former bookkeeper. The little sneak should remember that file. She tried to steal it."

Joe nodded. "We heard that she was dismissed under questionable circumstances."

"Yet she never tried to sue and clear her name," Frank said.

"We were wondering if there was anything you could tell us about that situation," Joe said.

Lamont's scowl disappeared as he nodded his head, impressed. He seemed to soften a little. "You two would make good investigative reporters—you already know quite a bit."

"Well, we've talked with Ms. Siegel," Frank said.

"I see," Lamont said. "And I'll bet that poor old lady told you how mean Clinton Lamont kicked her out of the company. So you come around here buttering me up to get some dirt about Old Glory. Well, if you want to become investigative reporters, go find someplace else to smear. This is a clean company. Nobody has ever believed otherwise."

"I don't—" Frank began.

Lamont cut him off. "Enough is enough. I want you two little snoops off these grounds."

"But, Mr. Lamont—" Joe said.

The security man walked to the door. "Out," he said calmly, opening the door for them. "You have five minutes to be out that front gate. If you aren't out by then, I'll have you arrested for trespassing."

Frank and Joe got up and walked out of the office. Lamont slammed the door behind them.

The boys left the grounds in the van as quickly as they could. About a mile past the gate, Frank suddenly said, "Joe, slow down."

"What's the matter?" Joe said. "We're not even doing thirty."

Frank was too busy to look at the speedometer. He was leaning over behind Joe's seat, pointing to a little plastic box lying on the floor.

Joe glanced in the rearview mirror. "What is that?" he asked. "It wasn't here when we—'

"That's right," Frank said. "There's a little sign on this box that says Potassium Chlorate. That's an explosive compound that goes off whenever it gets a sharp blow. So let's slow down, nice and easy, until we can stop and get this out of the van.

They had just reached a hillcrest overlooking town. As they rolled downhill, they began to pick up speed.

"I don't know how to tell you this," Joe said, pumping the brake pedal, "but somebody's nicked our brake line. I don't think we *can* stop!"

7 Trapped!

Joe jockeyed the steering wheel while fighting with the gear stick. Downshifting the gears managed to slow the van a little. But the downhill roll still had them moving—and the first pothole they hit could be a disaster.

Frank gingerly picked up the container, then started opening the window.

"Is it a good idea for you to hold that thing?" Joe asked.

"No," Frank answered briefly. "But it's our only chance to get rid of it. Pull off the road."

As Joe swung them onto the grassy edge of the road, Frank threw the plastic container out the window. It hit a rock—and with a *crack!* the container shattered.

"Pretty impressive," Joe said as the van rolled to a halt. "Lucky we saw that demonstration with potassium chlorate in chemistry class. If that stuff had exploded in the van—"

"It wouldn't have done very much damage,"

Frank cut in, frowning. "A container full of potassium chlorate would have been dangerous. But look at that rock where it exploded." He pointed. "It's not touched at all."

"So what are you saying? That this was a joke?" Joe asked. "Cutting our brakes isn't my idea of funny."

"The firecracker in the trailer truck, the thermite under our van in the driveway, and now this," Frank said, thinking out loud. "All of them were kind of dangerous—but not *really* dangerous, if you get what I mean."

"Dangerous enough," Joe said. "But it's hard to understand *who's* behind it. When you warned me about the stuff back there, Lamont was the first one to come to my mind. But I'm having second thoughts about him. The guy is a lunatic about security at his plant. Why would he plant those bags of firecrackers and this stuff right in his own backyard?"

"So where does that lead you?" Frank asked.

"Well, Anna Siegel didn't have any warm feelings for Lamont. And no matter what she said in her personnel report, she doesn't seem crazy about the company, either." He paused. "And in fourteen years, she might have picked up some info on making explosives—enough to build a bomb, but not enough to know how *big* to make it."

"So," Frank said, "she's beginning to look more and more like a genuine suspect." He shook his head. "Well, I'd rather go on that than think that someone is just playing with us."

Joe nodded. "So, that's taken care of. Now we just have one problem. Our van is useless—how do we get home?"

The answer to his question came rolling over the hillcrest just then. A shiny new minibus passed them, then came to a stop. Painted on its side was the name Bayport Inn.

"Hey, guys," a cheery voice called from the driver's window. "Check out my new wheels."

The doors opened, and the round face of Chet Morton beamed out at them. He had an official-looking cap on his head and wore a green uniform that matched the paint job on the minibus. The Hardys had to stifle a laugh. Their friend was famous for his enormous appetite and his crazy antics.

"What's this all about?" Joe asked.

Chet said proudly, "You're looking at the new shuttle-bus driver for the Bayport Inn. I pick up hotel guests at the airport and drive them to the hotel. And vice versa, of course. In between trips, I get to read, have a snack, visit my pals—or give them a lift if their van conks out."

"Sounds great," Joe said.

They locked the van, climbed aboard the minibus, and headed for home. As soon as they were in the Hardy house, they went into the kitchen, where Chet headed straight for the refrigerator and took out some brownies.

Joe shook his head. "Help yourself, Chet."

"What's up, you guys?" Chet said through a mouthful of chocolate. "You don't look so good. Here, have a brownie—maybe it'll give you some energy."

"This is a problem that even brownies won't solve," Frank said. "We've got a case on our hands, and we don't know what our next step should be."

"For that matter," Joe said, "we're not even sure we have a case on our hands. All we know for certain is that somebody seems to want to blow us up."

"Hey, guys," Chet said while he poured a glass of milk, "tell me what you need. If ol' buddy Chet can't help, then nobody can."

"Okay, Chet," Joe said, laughing. "Help us out. Why does Clinton Lamont seem to hate us?"

"Where does Anna Siegel fit in?" Frank asked, joining in the game.

"Can Don Munder give us any more help than he already has?" Joe said.

"And finally," Frank added, "what about this Kevin Bailey?"

Chet grinned. He took a long slug of milk and sat down at the table.

"Now listen up, friends," he said. "I can't help you with Clinton Lamont. I've never heard of Anna Siegel. And I wouldn't give you any advice about a man whose last name rhymes with *blunder*. But if you're looking for Kevin Bailey, you've come to the right man."

Still smiling, Frank said, "What are you talking about, Chet?"

"Kevin Bailey is staying at the Bayport Inn," Chet said. "I drove him there myself, just this morning."

"From where?" Joe asked.

"That's a good question," Chet said. "Most of my pickups are at the airport, with an occasional call from the railroad station. Bailey was bailing out of a hotel. He'd been at the Marina Hotel for a few days, then decided he wanted to stay at the Bayport Inn. So I drove him from the competition to our place."

"And you're sure about the name?" Frank asked.

"Positive," Chet said.

"This could be very valuable information, Chet," Frank said. "Do you think you can find out what room Bailey is in?"

"For you guys," Chet said, "I could find out his favorite color, his place of birth, and his shoe size."

"His favorite color we can do without," Joe said. "But his room number would help."

"Will do," Chet said. "May I add that it's an honor to be helping you out on this case? There's just one thing—what exactly is going on?"

Frank and Joe gave him a quick rundown on

what had happened so far. "So, Chet," Frank ended, "the sooner you give us this information, the faster we can go about making some sense of this case."

Chet scooped up three more brownies from the plate on the table. "For the road," he said. "I'm on the case!" He marched toward the front door. Joe and Frank followed him out.

"Chet," Joe said, "if this thing pans out, you're in line for a steak dinner with all the trimmings."

"Restaurant of my choice or yours?" Chet asked.

"Yours," Frank said. "Go to it."

Chet jogged out to the minibus. He hopped in and started the engine. As he pulled away, he yelled out the window, "On the case!"

Frank was about to close the door when Joe saw a familiar car coming from the opposite direction. He walked out to the curb to meet Iola's car. Iola rolled down her window.

"Hi," Joe said. "You just missed your brother."

"I'm just glad he found a new refrigerator to raid," Iola said. "He's been home four times today—too much time between trips."

"Did you come to visit?" Joe asked, smiling.

"Sort of," she said, as she got out of the car. "I really came to give you this book."

Joe took it and read the cover. "*The Complete Book of Fireworks.* Where did you get this?"

"My dad," she said. "I told him about the feature you and Frank are working on, and he dug this book out of the den."

"Tell him we both said thanks," Joe said as they stepped inside the house. He leaned over and gave her a kiss on the cheek.

"You're welcome," she said, smiling.

"Hey," Joe said, "how's the azalea wreath coming along?"

"Great. The float's really starting to take shape," she said. "How are you two making out with the sabotage mystery?"

"Not terrific," Joe said. "Chet is checking something out for us right now. That might open up some leads."

"Let's hope so," she said. She looked at her watch. "I have to get going."

"Thanks for the book. Are we still on for that pizza this Friday with Frank and Callie?"

"Sure," Iola said. "Talk to you tonight."

After Iola left, Joe sat on the couch and thumbed through the book she'd given him. At one page he stopped thumbing to look at a photograph. Then he read the page opposite the picture. He kept reading until the phone rang a half hour later.

"Joe?" a voice whispered into the line.

Joe remembered Frank's mystery caller. "What do you want now?"

"Bailey is in room two-thirty-three," the voice whispered.

Joe stared at the phone. "Who is this?"

"It's Chet!" The whisperer sounded a little hurt.

"Oh—and you found out Bailey is in room two-thirty-three," Joe said. "But why are you whispering?"

"Makes it more exciting," Chet said in his normal voice. "Don't you think so?"

Joe shook his head—typical Chet. "I guess so," he said, laughing. "Listen, are you going to be at the hotel for a while?"

"Yep," Chet said. "I don't have another run for over an hour."

"What's the possibility of our getting into Bailey's room?"

There was silence on the other end of the phone.

"Chet?"

"I'm here. Your question caught me a little off guard. I don't do this kind of thing every day, you know."

"Well, neither do we," Joe said.

"Okay. You and Frank get yourselves down here. I'll see to it that you get in there."

"Thanks. We'll be right over."

Joe and Frank borrowed their father's car. When they pulled up at the Bayport Inn, Chet came out of the lobby. Joe rolled down the passenger window.

"Bailey rented a car when he came in," Chet told them. "He drove off about ten minutes ago."

"Good," Joe said. "Now, how do we get into his room?"

"The best way," Chet explained, "is to use a passkey from one of the chambermaid's carts."

Frank asked, "You mean those things they use to deliver sheets and towels?"

"Right," Chet said. "The maids just finished the first level a while ago. That means they should be around Bailey's room just about now."

"How do you think we should do it?" Frank asked.

Chet looked pleased at being asked for advice. "Go to the second level. Just pretend you have a room on that floor. Wait until the maid goes into two-thirty or two-thirty-one. Then slide the key from the cart, open two-thirty-three, and slip inside."

"Got it," Joe said.

"I have to get back inside," Chet said. "Be careful, you guys—if you're caught, I'm dead."

"Right," Frank said. "And thanks, Chet."

Chet grinned and headed quickly back into the lobby.

Frank and Joe parked the car and walked into the hotel. They took the stairs to the second floor. A chambermaid was just coming out of room 229. She seemed to pay them no attention as they walked casually past her.

They reached the end of the hall and turned around. The chambermaid had already disappeared into room 231. Frank and Joe went quickly back the way they had come. Frank stopped at the door of room 233. Joe went several steps farther and stopped at the linen cart.

He walked around the cart, looking on each shelf. Finally, he spotted the key. He slid it off its hook and tossed it to Frank. Frank unlocked the door and tossed the key back to Joe, who put it back on its hook.

Seconds later, they were both inside the room. Bailey had obviously had takeout pizza for lunch—a box full of crusts sat on a table. He'd also changed—dirty clothes were strewn all over the floor and the bed. The smell of stale cigarette smoke hung in the air.

"He certainly keeps a nice place," Joe said.

"We aren't here to examine his housekeeping habits," Frank said. "Let's see if we can find anything that'll tell us why Bailey is in town."

Frank went to the dresser, and Joe lifted up the pizza box. Under it he found a pad of stationery. Each sheet had the name Northern Lights at the top.

Frank carefully moved the items on the dresser. He stopped when he came to a smaller pad. "Joe," he said, "look at this."

Joe stepped over to the dresser, where Frank was pointing to the pad. The top sheet had a note that Bailey had obviously written to himself. It said, "Meet Lamont 11 P.M."

Joe carefully placed the pizza box back where it had been. Frank moved the items on the dresser back to their original positions.

"Bailey definitely works for Northern Lights," Frank said.

"And he definitely has some business with Lamont," Joe added.

"It's time to get out of here," Frank said.

They moved to the door—then froze.

Someone was putting a key into the lock. In a second, the door would open—and they'd be caught!

8 I Read You Loud and Clear

As the key slid into the lock on room 233, Joe grabbed Frank's arm, pulling him to the window.

"We're two stories up—we can't jump!" Frank whispered as his brother opened the window.

"There's a ledge out there. Come on, it's our only hope."

Together, the boys scrambled onto the ledge, inching out of sight of the window just as the door swung open. They stood, their backs to the wall, looking straight ahead. "I hope they built this thing good and solid," Frank said. "What do we do if that's Bailey and he decides to spend the rest of the day in his room?"

"I'll sneak a peek through the window and see what's going on," Joe said. "Don't go away."

"Very funny." Frank gave his brother an evil look as Joe eased back to the window and looked in.

"That's a relief," Joe whispered.

"What?"

"It's only the chambermaid."

"Great news," Frank said. "But how's that going to get us off this ledge?"

"Relax and enjoy the view," Joe said. "You saw how quickly she did the room next door. Give her a couple of minutes. Then we'll slip back inside and walk out. Remember, this time the lock is on our side of the door."

He leaned over and peered into the room again. "She's putting sheets on the bed," he said. "She works fast."

"There's another way of looking at it," Frank whispered.

"What's that?"

"The Bayport Inn doesn't kill itself to keep the rooms clean."

Joe put his finger to his lips as the chambermaid came to the window. She ran a cloth over the frame, straightened out the drapes, and turned back into the room.

When they heard her walking away, Joe leaned over again to look inside.

"Now what?" Frank asked.

"Clean towels in the bathroom," Joe said. "She should be leaving soon." Then, after a pause, "Oh, no!"

He straightened up and flattened himself against the wall.

"What is it?" Frank whispered.

"Bailey's back."

They listened while Bailey moved around the room. Soon, they smelled cigarette smoke as it drifted out the window. Then they heard Bailey say, "Outside line, please."

"What's—" Frank began, but Joe signaled for him to be quiet.

"Everything is set for tomorrow night," Bailey said. Then he hung up the phone.

They heard him walking around, then came the welcome sounds of the door being unlocked, opened, and pulled shut. They stood frozen still for a full minute before Joe dared to lean over again. He looked into the room, then straightened up.

"No sign of him," he said.

"Could he be in the bathroom?" Joe asked.

"I don't think so. You heard the room door close."

They waited on the ledge a little longer, just in case. Then Joe said, "Let's try it."

He inched toward the window, which the chambermaid had left slightly open. Reaching out his foot, he slid the window open all the way. Then he eased himself into the room.

Frank followed quickly, and Joe moved toward the door. The bathroom was empty. Now they both stood at the locked door.

"He could be in the hall, you know," Joe said.

"I know," Frank said. "But I don't want to go out on that ledge again. Let's go."

Joe unlocked the door and slowly turned the handle. When the door was open, he leaned out and looked up and down the hall.

"Come on!" he said. Frank followed him out, pulling the door shut behind him. They walked—almost trotted—to the stairway, and made their way quickly down to the main floor.

Chet was loading luggage into the minibus just outside the main entrance. When he saw the Hardys, he gave them a small smile of relief. They returned the smile and walked across the street to their car.

On the way home, Frank repeated what Bailey had said. " 'Everything is set for tomorrow night.' What do you think he meant by that?"

"I don't know," Joe said. "We're still two days from the fireworks show. If he's talking about sabotage, he won't be doing it tomorrow night. I think we'd better change our tactics."

"What do you mean?" Frank asked.

"We have reason to believe that someone is planning to wreck the show. Lamont looks like a good suspect. And that memo in Bailey's room told us there's some kind of link between the two of them. There's also a good possibility that Siegel may have something to do with all this. I think we should start tailing them. Separately."

"Not a bad idea," Frank said. "But how can two of us tail *three* people?"

"No need to tail both Lamont and Bailey. If they're in this together, we only have to follow one of them."

"Good thinking," Frank said. "I'll stay outside the Old Glory grounds and watch for Lamont."

"Let's go home and get the motorcycles," Joe said. "I'll shadow Siegel."

Frank drove home and parked the car. He and Joe hopped out and headed for the garage. "We'll use the transceivers," Joe said.

They put on their new motorcycle helmets, rigged with radio transmitters and receivers. Joe adjusted the tiny microphone so it was in front of his mouth. Frank went into the house. Seconds later, Joe heard Frank's voice on his headset.

"Fearless Frank to GI Joe," he joked. "Do you read me?"

"Loud and clear," Joe said. "Do me a favor—read me the address on Anna Siegel's file, then let's get going."

Frank gave him the address, and Joe hopped on his motorcycle. As he was turning the corner, he saw Frank heading in the opposite direction. Joe took a shortcut to Anna Siegel's house, cutting about a mile off the four-mile trip. When he was a block away, he slowed down and looked for a parking space.

After he parked the motorcycle between two cars, he spoke into his mike. "GI Joe looking for Fearless Frank," he said.

His speaker crackled with static for a few seconds. Then he heard Frank's voice. "Fearless Frank coming back for the GI," it said.

"I'm at the target spot," Joe said, keeping his eye on the apartment house where Anna Siegel lived.

"I'm over here at Big Boom," Frank said. He was sitting outside the Old Glory grounds, waiting for Lamont.

"Let's keep the channel clear." Joe said. "Call only if you have something to report or to ask. Ten-four."

"Ten-four," Frank said, letting Joe know he'd received the message.

Joe had parked about fifty feet from the entrance to Siegel's building. There was a light on in her apartment.

On the other side of town, Frank was parked in a clump of trees near the Old Glory entrance. He could see the entrance, but no one would be able to see him without trying very hard to find him.

"GI Joe to Fearless Frank. We may have some action."

"What is it, GI?"

"My target's on the move," Joe said as he watched Siegel come out of her building. She got into a car parked several feet from the entrance and drove off.

"The target is moving on wheels," Joe said into his microphone. "And not driving very well. I'll get back to you. Ten-four." He started his motorcycle.

Joe hung back three or four car lengths behind Siegel. He wished now he was in a car—he'd be easy to spot on a motorcycle. Anna Siegel sped up ahead of him, then abruptly rounded a corner without signaling. Had he been spotted already?

Joe turned the corner to find Siegel chugging slowly down the street. She really was a lousy driver. "GI Joe looking for Fearless Frank," he said into the microphone. "We're now heading south on Brewster Drive."

"Don't take your eyes off the target, GI," Frank said.

"How are things at Big Boom?"

"Quiet. Don't worry about this end. Just keep your eye on her."

"Ten-four," Joe said.

Several minutes later, Siegel pulled up in front of the Bayport Inn. Joe pulled into the lot across the street where he and Frank had parked their father's car earlier.

Joe leaned against his bike and watched

Siegel, who sat in her car and watched the hotel entrance. Five minutes passed, then seven, then ten. Finally, a man dressed in a raincoat and hat came out of the hotel. He spotted Siegel's car and got in.

Joe fumbled with his mike. "GI Joe to Fearless Frank," he said excitedly.

"Go for Fearless," Frank said.

"A second target has just come up to the vehicle."

"Where are you?"

"Same place we were this afternoon."

"Are they moving?"

"No. They're getting out. I'll get back to you. Ten-four."

He watched as Siegel and the man left the car, heading for the hotel coffee shop. Joe strolled from the motorcycle in the direction of the coffee shop. All he wanted right now was a look at the man with Siegel—without the coat and hat in the way.

On the other side of town, Frank stared at Old Glory's main building. At least something's happening with Joe, he thought. I may be here all night with nothing to report.

He stretched in a big yawn—just as Lamont came driving out. His short-cropped white hair was unmistakable. Frank gave him ten seconds, then started his engine and followed.

Lamont's route took them out of town. As he followed along a series of country roads, Frank saw the security man keep looking into his rearview mirrors. Finally, Lamont actually leaned out his window to eyeball Frank.

That left Frank no choice—he had to let Lamont get way ahead. Finally, about six miles from the plant, Lamont pulled into a driveway. Frank passed by as Lamont unlocked the front door and threw a light switch.

Stopping at the corner, Frank left his bike and headed back past the house. Lamont stood just inside the door, looking through a pile of mail. Then, taking off his coat, he closed the door.

The living room light went on. Frank watched through a picture window as Lamont flopped into a chair, picking up the remote control for his TV. The security man kicked off his shoes and sat back. In two minutes, he was asleep.

Frank was heading back to his cycle when a blast of static nearly deafened him.

"GI Joe to Fearless Frank." Joe's voice sounded excited.

"Go, GI."

"The targets are moving—and the man's driving. This isn't going to be—"

Then all Frank heard was static.

Frank yelled into his mike. "Don't hang me up like that, Joe. Hey, do you read me. Joe? Joe!"

As empty static continued to crackle in his ears, Frank revved his engine and screeched back to town.

9 Stakeout

Frank blasted his way through traffic, desperate to find out what had happened to his brother. It meant flirting with the speed limit, but he neared the Bayport Inn just nine minutes after Joe's radio had gone dead.

Two blocks from the hotel, he spotted Joe's bike, lying on its side under a tree. Frank gripped his hand brakes, screeching to a stop. Joe's helmet lay on the ground, a few yards from the bike.

"Hi, Frank," Joe called from the shadows under the tree. He lay in tall grass, leaning against the trunk.

"Joe!" Frank said. "What happened?"

Joe shook his head and winced. "I just took the bad-driving award from Anna Siegel. Guess I was too busy watching where she and her boyfriend were going, instead of watching the road." He pointed up. "That branch left me flat on my back."

Frank saw how the low-hanging branch could sweep someone off a bike.

"I was hanging back, so they didn't even see me go down." He sighed. "And I didn't see where they were headed." Grunting, he got to his feet.

"Are you hurt?" Frank asked.

"Just my . . . pride." Joe rubbed the seat of his jeans.

Frank checked out Joe's cycle, while Joe tested out his arms and legs. "Find out anything about Siegel and our mystery man?" Frank asked.

"Just that he wasn't Kevin Bailey," Joe said, climbing onto his cycle. "I was sure that's who she was meeting. But this was a guy I've never seen before."

"Maybe Chet can identify him from your description. Let's ask him about that—after we get home," Frank said. "We're not going to uncover anything else tonight."

Frank eased his cycle into the light nighttime traffic. Joe followed him, and they headed home.

A half hour later, Fenton Hardy joined his two sons in the kitchen as they reheated some supper leftovers. "How's that videotape coming, boys?" he asked.

Joe was about to speak, but Frank gave him a look. He wasn't quite ready to go public with a wild-sounding note and no—or was that too many?—solid suspects.

"Just fine, Dad," Frank jumped in. "We're going to start editing soon."

"Before the fireworks show?" Mr. Hardy asked.

"Well, yes," Frank said. "We know the show will fill the last minutes of the tape. Our problem is to edit everything else down so we don't go over seven minutes."

"Will we get to see it before it airs?" Mrs. Hardy asked.

"You know the right people," Joe said. "As soon as we're ready, make a batch of popcorn, and we'll have a private screening."

When the boys had finished their late supper, they called Chet and asked him to come over. Frank promised him a hefty share of leftovers.

Chet arrived, dressed in his bus driver's outfit. "Hello, Hardy family," he said, strolling through the front door.

He planted himself firmly at the kitchen table. Joe put a heaping plate of cold meat loaf, lima beans, and warmed-up mashed potatoes in front of him.

"Chet," Frank said, "we need a little more help. Joe saw a man come out of the Bayport Inn this evening—we hope you can identify him."

Chet swallowed a mouthful of potatoes. "What did he look like?"

"He was about six foot four," Joe said, "with long hair and a thick mustache."

Chet thought for a moment. "Sorry," he said. "That doesn't sound like anyone I've seen at the inn."

Joe sat back in his chair, disappointed. "Are you up for a ride, Frank?" he asked.

"Where to?" Frank asked.

"To Anna Siegel's. I'm still kicking myself for losing her before. Maybe we'll catch her coming back home. If we're really lucky, the guy will be with her."

"It doesn't sound very hopeful," Frank said. "But I'll give it a try, sure."

They stood up and moved toward the doorway. Chet swallowed his food and wiped his mouth with a napkin.

"Can I come along, guys?" he said. "Maybe if I saw this guy, it would jog my memory."

"Sure," Frank said. "But don't expect anything exciting to happen."

"Or even interesting, for that matter," Joe added.

Chet managed a final mouthful of meat loaf while Joe borrowed his father's car keys. Chet took the shotgun seat while Joe drove.

"Where are we going?" he asked.

"The Bayport Gardens apartment complex," Frank said, climbing into the backseat.

Chet flipped the switch on the radio and got the police band. When he heard the voice of a police dispatcher, he grinned. "I was going for music, but I guess this is better background for a stakeout."

"It isn't a stakeout, Chet," Joe said, turning to face him from behind the wheel. "We just want to make sure our suspects are accounted for."

"Sounds like a stakeout to me," Chet insisted.

A few minutes later, Joe pulled up near the entrance to Siegel's building. Once again, her light was on. She was sitting near the window, reading a newspaper or a magazine.

"She seems to be safely tucked away," Joe said.

"Let's take Chet to see the other main suspect," Frank said.

Joe turned the car around and followed Frank's directions to Lamont's house. When they arrived, Lamont's living room light was still on. They could see him asleep in his easy chair.

"I don't think he's moved a muscle since I left him," Frank said.

"Chet," Joe said, "this might give you a taste of what real detective work is like—about ninety-eight percent drudgery and boredom."

"Mostly nothing but dead ends and blind alleys," Frank said.

The police radio crackled with static. "Assistance needed at Old Glory fireworks plant," the voice said.

Joe leapt at the dial and raised the volume.

"Cars seventeen, thirty-six, and twelve, proceed to Old Glory fireworks plant on Mill Valley Road. Four-seven-three reported at Old Glory plant."

Joe had already started the engine and was moving the van down the street.

"Four-seven-three," Frank said. "That's a break-in."

They followed the same route Lamont had taken from the plant earlier that night. Joe slowed at the gate, then saw that the guard's post was empty. He drove on, homing in on the flashing red lights of four police cars. Police officers surrounded the main office building, shining flashlights. Joe had already cut his headlights, rolling the car to a stop beyond the edge of the police activities.

He and Frank hopped out. "Chet," Joe said, "maybe you should wait here."

Chet nodded silently. The police investigation looked exciting, but he wasn't sure he wanted to be any closer than he was right now.

Frank and Joe looked around. "Half the night shift must be here," Joe said, indicating the squad cars.

Frank said, "Let's see if we can find out what happened."

They walked slowly toward the crowd gathered outside the main building. Then they both spotted Don Munder at the same time. He was talking to two police officers. Frank and Joe moved closer so they could hear what he was saying.

"At least three offices were vandalized," Munder said, "maybe more. I didn't have a chance to look everywhere."

"Was one of the offices yours, sir?" a police officer asked.

"Yes, it was," Munder said.

"Anything missing?"

"There doesn't appear to be," Munder said.

"Thank you, Mr. Munder," the officer said. "Give us some time to look around. We may need to talk to you again when we're finished."

Munder spotted Frank and Joe. He motioned for them to join him.

"Are you all right?" Frank asked him.

"I'm fine," he said.

"What happened?" Joe asked.

"Come with me," Munder said. They followed him to a spot behind the building and away from the crowd.

"My office was trashed, along with at least two others," Munder said. "And there's only one person who could get into all three—Clinton Lamont."

"Maybe so, Mr. Munder," Frank said. "But he isn't the one who did this."

"And just how do you know that?" Munder asked.

"We happen to know where he is right now," Frank said. "And, for that matter, where he's been for the last several hours."

"Is that a fact?" Munder frowned. "Well, I'm not suggesting that he actually did the damage himself."

"What are you suggesting?" Joe asked.

"That he may have had some help."

"Help?" Frank said. "Help from whom?"

"Kevin Bailey," Munder said. "One of our ex-employees. He was with Lamont the night you were taping out here."

Frank and Joe looked at each other. They each knew what the other was thinking.

"We should tell the police about this," Joe said.

"Not if you're going to quote me as a source," Munder said. "I need this job. No way am I accusing a powerful man like Lamont. Quote me, and I'll deny I told you anything at all."

Frank and Joe returned to the front of the building, where they were glad to see the familiar face of Con Riley.

"Hey, Con," Joe called.

Con turned to them and nodded. He walked past Chief Collig and joined the boys.

"We have some information that may be of help," Joe said.

"Thanks, guys," Con said. "But I have some real police work to do here."

Frank said, "Does that mean you don't want to hear what we know about this break-in?"

Con eyed Frank with a look of interest and amusement. He realized that more than once the Hardys had picked up information before the police had. He thought for a moment, then said, "Okay. What is it?"

"Lamont may have been responsible for what happened here tonight," Frank said.

Con chuckled. "That's very interesting, Frank. Now I have to get back to work."

"You don't believe us?" Joe asked.

"Normally, I probably would," Con said. "But not this time. It just so happens that we had to rouse Lamont from a deep sleep to get him here tonight. I sent a car to his house just after we got here. He's on his way here right now."

"He may have an accomplice or two," Joe said.

"What are you talking about?" Con asked.

"There's someone in town from Massachusetts," Frank said. "We have reason to believe that he's working with Lamont."

"Working at what?" Con asked.

"We're not completely sure," Joe said. "But we think it has something to do with messing up the Founders' Day celebration."

"Why would Lamont want to do that to his own employer?" Con asked.

"We aren't sure about that yet, either," Frank said. "But our information comes from a reliable source."

A police car with flashing lights pulled up to the main building. The boys watched Lamont climb out of the backseat, looking tired and angry.

"Wait right here," Con told Joe and Frank. "I'll be back."

Con approached Lamont. Frank and Joe watched as the two men talked. They wondered just what Con was saying.

But they had no doubt about Lamont's reaction. If the scene were in a cartoon, Joe thought, smoke would be coming out of Lamont's ears right now. His face was turning red, and he clenched his fists so tightly his nails must have cut into his palms.

The boys stepped closer. They heard Lamont's response to what Con had just said.

"This theory of yours, Officer Riley," Lamont said, "it wouldn't have anything to do with those kid reporters over there, would it?"

Con tilted his head but didn't answer.

"Why in the name of Sam Hill would I sabotage my own company?" Lamont roared. Then he walked toward a police officer who was standing near Frank and Joe.

"Officer," he said, "these boys have no reason to be on this property. Would you please escort them through the front gate?"

The officer looked at Con Riley. "Do as he says," Con said. "In fact, see that they get home safely."

"That's one problem handled," Lamont said to Con. "Next, I get to chew out the assistant who's in charge of security for this shift." He walked off to where Lew Collins was standing at the edge of the police activity and grabbed the young man's arm.

Frank and Joe kept the car between them and Lamont as they walked back.

Chet, still sitting in the front seat, said, "Wow, what did you do to that guy? He sounds really mad."

"He's just all-around bad news," Frank said, getting into the driver's seat and starting the car. "I wonder what he's telling Lew Collins."

"The young guy in the blue jacket? I heard part of it." Chet suddenly looked a lot more serious. "In fact, it might have been about you two."

He looked from Frank to Joe in the backseat. Then Chet said, "He said, 'It's time to do something about those two—permanently.'"

10 Evidence on the Videotape

"Permanently." Chet said again, and looked nervously at Frank, who was driving. "You don't think he's going to try to—uh—kill you guys, do you?"

Frank thought of all the bombs that had gone off around them lately. "Well, I don't think he'd try it tonight, Chet—not when we have a police escort."

Chet turned in his seat to watch the police car behind them. "They're following us?"

"Thanks to Clinton Lamont," Joe said. "It sounds like we've got him running a little scared."

Frank nodded. "Maybe we're finally getting somewhere on this sabotaging of Founders' Day—and maybe he's getting a little nervous."

"No kidding?" Chet said. "But why sabotage Founders' Day?"

"That's one of the things we have to find out," Joe said. "And not only why, but how."

Frank eased the car into the driveway of the Hardy house. The police car drove past. Joe grinned. "Hey, Frank, you didn't wave good-bye."

The three of them got out of the car, Chet grabbing his bus driver's cap and putting it on his head. His own car was parked in front of the house.

"Well," he said, walking toward his car, "that's probably enough excitement for me for one night."

Frank laughed. "What did you think of the stakeout, Chet?" he asked.

"It wasn't the most fun I've had lately," he said, getting into his car. "But somehow, it's made me hungry. I hope my folks didn't eat all the rum-raisin ice cream in the freezer." He looked at the Hardys. "If I can help you guys with any more information, give me a call. Otherwise, I'm going to leave the legwork to you."

Frank and Joe waved as Chet drove off. They went into the house, fell onto the sofa, and sat silently for a while.

Finally, Frank said, "So what do we do now?"

"We know Lamont is going to do the job, one

way or another," Joe said. "And it seems pretty certain that Bailey is going to help him."

"But we still don't have a motive—or a method," Frank said. "In fact, when you get right down to it, we don't even know what they might do. Are they going to blow up the building? Deactivate the fireworks on Saturday night? Throw tomatoes at the people in the parade on Sunday?"

"I think we can safely rule out the last possibility," Joe said. "No tomato thrower would have sent us a gift of thermite, or put a little potassium chlorate in our van."

"I guess you're right," Frank said. "Yeah, we do have something serious on our hands. I wish we knew just how serious it was."

They sat in silence again, thinking over what had happened that day. Then Frank said, "I have to go to WBPT in the morning. I think I'll call Phil and ask him to meet me there. I want to discuss lighting with him."

The next morning, Frank picked up the repaired van, loaded the videotapes aboard, and drove to WBPT. The station was near the center of town, in a large, white building. It had been built as the headquarters of a new television network. The network had failed, but WBPT was still on the air. Frank drove past the enormous satellite receiving dish in front of the building and parked near the main entrance.

"Hi, Ruth," he greeted the receptionist as he carried his tapes inside.

"Morning, Frank," she said. "I have editing room four reserved for you."

"Thanks," Frank said. "Oh, by the way, a friend of mine is going to be working with me today. Phil Cohen. When he gets here, can you just send him back?"

"Sure thing," Ruth said.

Frank walked past the studio and the newsroom. At the end of a short hallway was a group of small editing rooms, each packed with state-of-the-art video equipment. Editing room four had several VCRs, four television monitors, two videotape recorders—and barely enough room for Frank to get in.

He took off his jacket and sat down. Then he put one of the Old Glory tapes into a VCR, but before he had a chance to press the play button, there was a knock at the door. Frank reached out, opened the door, and saw Phil standing in the hall.

"Hey, Phil," Frank said. "Come on in."

Phil looked the editing room up and down. "Look at all this equipment," he said. "There isn't anything you couldn't do in this room."

"With all this hardware," Frank said slowly, "I still don't have a clue about what's going down on Saturday."

"Checking out the Old Glory tapes?" Phil asked, taking off his jacket.

"Yeah," Frank said. "I have to get them edited together as a rough cut. After I've put together all the tape we'd like to show, we'll see how long it runs—and start cutting back." He sighed. "I also thought I'd run the tapes for you. Maybe you'll catch something that Joe and I missed."

"You guys still tracking down that sabotage theory?" Phil asked.

"Yeah," Frank said. "We may have someone nailed down, but we don't know what kind of trouble he plans to cause."

"There are a lot of things he could do with fireworks," Phil said. "When you're playing with explosives, sabotage becomes pretty easy."

"Why don't you run some of those things by me?" Frank said.

"Well," Phil said, "have you considered the worst possible case?"

"I'm not sure," Frank said. "What do you think that is?"

"He could blow up the *Barbary Blood,"* Phil said.

"How much damage would that do?"

"My guess is that we could say goodbye to the marina and everyone even close to the water. On Founders' Day, that could mean pretty near the whole town."

"That's a pretty horrible picture," Frank said. "But I don't think it's a real possibility. It looks like this guy is after Old Glory—maybe put them out of business. But I don't think he'd target most of the population of Bayport."

"Well, then," Phil said, "how about this? If all this guy wants is Old Glory out of the picture, maybe he'll just try to keep the fireworks from going off."

"Somehow, that sounds a little too tame for the character Joe and I have been dealing with."

"Are you sure?" Phil said. "What better way to embarrass a fireworks company than to make sure its products fizzle?"

"I guess that's true," Frank said. But he was thinking of the various presents he and Joe had received from their anonymous enemy. "I think we're facing something more dangerous than that, though."

Phil shrugged. "Let's take a look at the tapes."

Frank pressed the play button on the VCR. They watched as the camera panned around the inside of one of the dugouts where the Old Glory explosives were stored. After a while, Phil stopped the tape and reversed it. Then he pressed the play button again.

"What are you looking at?" Frank asked.

"Wait," Phil said. "It's just another few seconds. There! Look at this, Frank."

Phil pressed the freeze button to create a still picture of the stockpile.

"I'm looking," Frank said. "But all I see are

the artillery shells they'll be using to fire off the rockets for the fireworks display."

"Look a little more closely," Phil said, staring at the picture frozen on the screen. "What do you see there?" He picked up a pencil and held it to the corner of the screen.

"That doesn't look like a fun firework to me. And why would they need it on the ship?"

Frank moved his head closer to the screen. He could see a reddish brown stick peeking out from behind the pile of shells. Only three inches showed, but the thing had to be about a foot long.

"That's dynamite!" he told Phil.

"Well, it's not just a big firecracker," Phil said. "We may have found out what your suspect has up his sleeve."

Frank stopped the tape and ejected it from the machine. "That's quite an eye you have there, Cohen," he said.

Phil shrugged. "It's all those circuit boards I play with. If you're going to spot a broken wire, you've got to look pretty hard."

"I'd better call Joe and tell him about this," Frank said as he walked Phil out to the parking lot.

"I'd be extra careful if I were you," Phil said. "I'd hate to look at the front page of the *Times* and see a headline that says, 'Young Detective Blown to Kingdom Come.'"

"Not to worry, my friend," Frank said. "Joe and I are pretty explosive guys ourselves."

When Phil had left, Frank went back into the studio and called Joe. "Get down here right away," he said. "Phil just discovered something on one of our tapes that I know you'll want to see."

Joe arrived ten minutes later. While Frank was showing him the tape that revealed the hidden dynamite, they heard a commotion in the hallway. They left the editing room and followed the sounds to the newsroom.

"What's up, Barney?" Frank asked one of the cameramen.

"Hot story," Barney said, sounding bored. "The boss wants a crew out at the Old Glory fireworks plant."

Frank and Joe look startled. "What for?" Joe asked.

"Some kind of accident," Barney said.

"Come on," Frank said, "we'll follow them in the van."

The boys followed the camera crew out of the building. Then they got into their van, Joe in the driver's seat.

"I have an idea for a new feature for WBPT news," Joe said as he pulled out and followed the news truck.

"What's that?" Frank asked.

"A news update on the hour," Joe said.

"They already have that."

"Not the one I'm thinking of," Joe said. "This update would be strictly for trouble at

Old Glory. Then, at night, they could have a summary of all the day's problems."

Frank gave him a look. "Very cute."

Barney drove through the factory's entrance gate, and the Hardy van followed him in. The scene at the main building was chaos. The entrance to the building was blocked by at least six police cars, two fire trucks, a truck from the bomb squad, and an ambulance. The mobile units from three television stations took up whatever space was left.

Frank and Joe jumped out of the van and stood in the middle of the commotion. They spotted Con Riley, then made their way through the crowd until they'd caught up with him.

"What are you two doing here?" Con asked, obviously not very happy to see them.

"We're with the WBPT crew," Joe said. "What's happened?"

"That's for us to find out," Con said, not nearly as friendly as he usually was. "After last night, I would have thought you two would have more sense than to come back here."

"You're still sore about our sabotage theory, aren't you?" Frank said.

"I haven't got time to play games," Con said. "We've got a lot of damage here, and at least one ambulance case."

By listening to various reporters who had beaten them to the scene, Joe and Frank learned that Lamont's office had been vandalized. He'd returned to his office in time to see the culprit getting out a window. But he hadn't seen the booby trap the culprit had left. An explosive blast had seriously injured him.

The police forced everyone back from the entrance as two paramedics carried Lamont out on a stretcher. His head was covered with a loose bandage, and he was also bleeding from his right arm.

Barney hoisted the video camera onto his shoulder, while several other camera operators did the same. All lenses were focused on Lamont's bleeding face. He seemed conscious, but dazed.

Denise Fergus, the evening anchor for WBPT, called over the noise, "Mr. Lamont! Can you tell us anything about the intruders?"

Her microphone, and those of several others, were then pointed in the direction of the stretcher.

Lamont opened his eyes and looked around. He spotted Frank, who was standing near the back door of the ambulance. He motioned to one of the paramedics to stop. Then he weakly waved Frank to come to the stretcher.

Frank stepped closer and leaned over. "What is it, Mr. Lamont?" he asked.

"You were right," Lamont groaned.

Frank realized that several video cameras and microphones were trained on him and

Lamont. He held his hand near his mouth and leaned closer to whisper in Lamont's ear.

"You mean sabotage?"

Lamont nodded.

The security man clutched at Frank's arm, trying to say something else. But his voice failed. Lamont's lips moved—mouthing the word *murder*, Frank thought. Then Lamont passed out.

The two paramedics picked up the stretcher and carried it into the ambulance. Frank watched them go, wondering what it was Lamont had been trying to say about murder.

Joe was now standing at Frank's side. "What did he say?" he asked out of the corner of his mouth.

"He said we were right," Frank said, watching the ambulance pull away.

Joe thought for a moment. "But that means we were also wrong," he said.

"Yeah," Frank said. "Lamont obviously isn't trying to destroy anything."

"Then who is?" Joe asked.

"He tried to tell me. But he ran out of strength and passed out."

"Well," Joe said, "if it wasn't Lamont, then—"

"Anna Siegel!" Frank said. "Let's go find out how she's been spending her time for the past couple of hours."

They ran to the van and took off for Anna

Siegel's apartment house. In minutes, they were racing up the stairs to her apartment. Joe pounded on her door, while Frank rang the bell over and over. No response.

"What should we do?" Joe asked.

"I say we wait right here. If she isn't home in about an hour, we'll have to tell Con about her and let him take over."

Ten minutes later, Anna Siegel stepped off the elevator carrying a large box from the Bayport Bridal Shop. She jumped when she saw her two visitors.

"Oh, you frightened me!" she said. "What are you two doing here?"

"Waiting for you," Joe said.

"For me?" Siegel said. "Why?"

Frank said, "Because of what just happened out at Old Glory."

She looked puzzled. "What happened?" she asked. "And what could it possibly have to do with me?"

"Lamont's office was vandalized," Frank said. "And Mr. Lamont was hurt pretty badly by a booby trap."

She stared at them for several seconds. Then she said, "Do you seriously believe that I broke into the plant?"

"We're just checking out leads," Joe said. "Can you account for your time during the past two hours or so?"

"Of course I can!" she said hotly. "I've spent the past three and a half hours on the final fitting on a dress for my sister's wedding this weekend. And if you don't believe me, you can ask all of my relatives who are staying at the Bayport Inn."

"I'm sure that won't be necessary," Joe said, seeing both Anna Siegel and the mystery man from the inn being cleared of suspicion.

"If you'll excuse me," she said, "I'd like to get into my apartment."

"Yes, of course," Frank said, feeling frustrated at losing yet another suspect. This case seemed to be leading nowhere fast.

"Correct me if I'm wrong," Joe said as they walked away, "but this seems to leave us without a case."

"Oh, no," Frank said. His face was grim as he turned to his brother. "There's no mystery about *what's* going to happen. What scares me is not knowing *who's* going to make it happen —and how we can stop them."

11 Kevin Bailey, Suspect

Joe sat in his favorite booth at the Liberty Bell Diner, waiting for Frank to finish on the phone.

He was doodling on a placemat, writing *Lamont,* then scribbling over the name. Then he wrote *Siegel,* added a question mark, and scribbled over that. Next came *Collins* and *Munder* and more scribbles. Finally he wrote *Bailey,* drawing a circle of question marks around the name.

Frank hung up and came back to the booth. "Did they tell you anything?" Joe asked.

"Hospital people are always a little vague," Frank said. "But it sounds as though Lamont's going to be all right. He has a lot of cuts and bruises, but it's the concussion they're worried about."

"Can we talk to him?" Joe asked.

"Not a chance. They're waking him every few hours to make sure he doesn't slip into a coma. But they won't let anyone in to talk to him for at least three more days."

"In other words," Joe said, "not till the day after the celebration."

"And maybe the day after the disaster," Frank said glumly.

As they both began to eat, Chet came in. "Hey, guys, looks like I came at just the right time," he said, taking a couple of fries from Joe's plate. "Your aunt told me I'd find you here."

"Hi, Chet," Frank said as Chet sat across from him.

"You guys seem a little down," Chet said. No leads, huh?"

"Nothing we can make any sense of," Frank said. "A lot of attacks, but no suspects."

"I might be able to help you out with that," Chet said. "When I heard what happened over at Old Glory on the radio, I checked up on your friend Bailey. He was out of his room when it happened."

"Are you sure?" Joe asked.

"Yes," Chet said. "The desk clerk saw him leave a little before one o'clock."

"That would give him nearly an hour to get to Old Glory," Joe said. "More than enough time."

"I'll be shuttling between the airport and

the hotel the rest of the day," Chet said. "If there's anything I can do for you, leave a message at the hotel." He grabbed the rest of Joe's fries. "Thanks, pal."

"Thank *you*, Chet," Frank said. Through the window, he watched Chet get into the minibus and drive away.

"What now?" Joe asked.

"It's back to the editing room for me," Frank said. "I haven't gotten anything done on the tape. Every time I start, something comes up and I have to leave. I'm going down there now."

"Okay," Joe said. "Drop me off at home first."

They got into the van and pulled out of the parking lot. Frank dropped his brother at home.

"I'll be back in a few hours," he said.

Joe went inside and found that no one was home. He sprawled out on the couch and picked up the book Iola had given him.

"*The Complete Book of Fireworks,*" he read aloud. He opened to the table of contents. "Disasters," he read. "Page sixty-eight."

He turned to page sixty-eight, where he saw a full-page picture of a brick building that had been knocked flat by an explosion. The text on the opposite page told him that, while accidents at fireworks plants were rare, when they did happen, they caused much destruction.

Joe thought about the crowds at a typical Founders' Day celebration. The idea of an "accident" taking place made him shudder.

An hour later, the jangling telephone woke Joe with a start. He jumped from the couch, took a second to decide where he was, then walked to the other side of the room and answered the phone.

"Hello," he said groggily.

"Junior Detective Morton here," said the voice on the other end.

"Junior? . . . Oh, hi, Chet."

"I have some more fun facts for you," Chet said.

"Well? Come on!" Joe said impatiently.

"Bailey has a phone message waiting for him—from Anna Siegel. She wants to meet him."

Joe's eyes widened. "Now that's what I call a tip!" he said. "Do you know when? And where?"

"I do," Chet said. "What kind of junior detective would I be without the whole scoop? Seven tonight, outside Kelp's Restaurant," Chet said.

"Kelp's?" Joe asked. "On pier fourteen?"

"That's right," Chet said.

"Thanks, Chet."

Joe hung up the phone, let it sit for two seconds, and picked it up again. He dialed WBPT and asked for the editing rooms.

"Frank," he said, "get over here right away. Chet just told me that Siegel and Bailey are meeting tonight at seven."

"Be home in fifteen minutes," Frank said.

Joe hung up and lifted the phone again. This time he dialed Phil's number.

"Phil," he said, "Joe Hardy here. Do you still have that long-range microphone we used to use at football games?"

"Sure," Phil said. "It's packed away in the garage."

"Can you unpack it and get it over here right away?"

"Be there in half an hour," Phil said.

Joe hung up the phone and rubbed his hands together. At last, maybe they were going to see some action.

He walked into the kitchen and opened the refrigerator door. Then he closed it. Then he opened it and closed it again. He sat at the table and drummed his fingers. Then he decided to wait for Frank outside.

When the van turned the corner, Joe ran to meet it. Frank parked in front of the house and got out of the van. "Pretty worked up, aren't you?" he said, laughing.

"They're getting together!" Joe said. "This is the break we've been waiting for!"

"Maybe," Frank said. "What else do we know?"

"Seven o'clock in front of Kelp's on Pier

Fourteen," Joe said. "I envision an outdoor conversation. So I called Phil and told him we need his long-range mike."

"Good thinking," Frank said, leading the way into the house.

Ten minutes later, they heard a car pull into their driveway. Phil came into the house, carrying a black leather case. He put it on the living room floor and opened it.

"What kind of range does it have?" Frank asked.

"I used to get about two hundred feet with it," Phil said, screwing the head of the mike onto the body. "But that was at football games, with a lot of crowd noise. You should get more distance."

"We can park across from Kelp's," Joe said.

"What are you using it for?" Phil asked.

"Two of our suspects are getting together tonight," Frank said. "There's a chance they'll be talking outdoors."

"If they do," Phil said, "this should do the trick."

"How does it work?" Frank asked.

"Just aim and listen," Phil said. "Use this connection here to hook it up to your tape recorder."

After Phil left, Joe and Frank spent an hour trying the mike out. Joe stood in front of the house, and Frank talked from 200 feet, then 300 feet, then 350 feet. At 400 feet, the mike could still pick up his normal voice, but it began to lose his whispers. The boys were amazed at how sensitive the microphone was.

At six-thirty, they drove to Pier 14 and parked across from Kelp's. Frank sat in the passenger's seat, the microphone in his lap. The tape recorder rested on the floor behind Joe's seat.

Five minutes later, Anna Siegel drove into Kelp's parking lot. She got out of her car, walked to the pier, and stood looking out at the bay.

A large, white car pulled into the parking lot. The door opened, and Bailey stepped out.

Frank and Joe each put on a pair of headphones. Frank switched the mike on, which started the tape running. Then he rolled his window down and pointed the mike in the direction of the pier.

Siegel turned and saw Bailey walking toward her. They shook hands.

"Here we go," Joe said.

"Hello, Kevin," Siegel said.

"Good to see you, Anna," Bailey said. "I was surprised to get your call."

"It's high time we talked," Siegel said.

Bailey turned toward the restaurant. "Shall we go in?"

"No!" Joe whispered desperately.

"I'd like to talk in private," Anna Siegel said. "We can sit in your car."

"Annie," Joe begged, "don't do it!"

"Fine," Bailey said.

Frank took his headphones off and looked at his brother. "The mike won't work through a car door," Joe said.

Frank put the headset back on and looked out at Bailey's car. Bailey and Siegel were talking. But nothing was coming through to the mike.

"We have to hear what they're saying in there!" Joe said, his voice panicky.

Frank stared steely-eyed at the big, white car. "Suppose I go over and ask if we could join them?" he said. "Somehow, I don't think they'll like the idea."

The Hardys both gazed glumly at the car. Joe fiddled with his headset, as though that might magically bring in the sounds he was desperate to hear. The mike was still pointed at the car, but all it picked up were some street sounds.

Frank turned to him. "I guess we might as well go home." He pulled off his headset and dropped it into his lap.

Joe's eyes widened. He clasped his hands over his headset and said, "Listen!"

Frank turned to look at the car. Bailey had rolled his window down. His left arm extended out the window. In his hand was a lighted cigarette. Frank put his headset on. Then he turned to make sure the tape recorder was running.

"I met with him a few nights ago," Bailey

said. "I've applied to Pembroke Industries for a job, and I needed a reference. Clint knows the president of Pembroke."

Frank turned and looked at Joe. This wasn't exactly what they had expected to hear.

Bailey's hand moved inside the window. Seconds later, it came out again, followed by a puff of cigarette smoke.

"You heard what happened today?" Siegel asked.

"Yes. I saw it on the news."

"I was never a big fan of Lamont's," Siegel said. "But that booby trap really disturbed me. He looked pretty badly hurt."

"Yes, he did," Bailey said. "I tried to get in to see him at the hospital, but they said he wouldn't be able to have visitors for days."

"I did something I never would have believed I'd do," Siegel said.

"What's that?"

"I sent flowers to Clinton Lamont."

Bailey chuckled. "I'm sure he'll be surprised when he finally sees your name on the card," he said.

Frank turned to look at Joe, who rolled his eyes to show his frustration.

"Sounds like we've cut in on a tea party of Aunt Gertrude's," Frank said.

"Will you be around for the festivities?" Siegel asked.

"No," Bailey said. "I have to get back to the

home office. Besides, I saw enough of these shows when I was working here."

"Listen," she said, "I owe you an apology."

"Apology?" he said. "What have you done?"

"I haven't done anything," she said. "But I've been harboring some pretty nasty suspicions about you and Clinton."

"Do I dare ask what kind of suspicions?"

"They all seem pretty silly now," she said. "I thought you and he were cooking something up. I thought maybe you'd persuaded him to do some corporate spying for Northern Lights or something."

"Corporate spying?" Bailey laughed loudly. "Clinton Lamont? I'd like to meet the guy who could convince Lamont to do something like that. Somebody that persuasive could get a monkey elected president."

"I guess you're right," she said, laughing. "After he got me fired, I just let myself be blinded by anger. Maybe it's time to get past that."

"The flowers were a good start," he said.

"I'll call Clint next week," she said. "It's probably about time that he and I buried the hatchet."

"It's been good talking to you, Anna," Bailey said. "Sorry I didn't have more time. I have to get going. I have a long drive ahead of me."

"It was good seeing you again," Siegel said.

When the car door opened, Frank pulled the

mike inside his window. Siegel got out of the car, and she and Bailey exchanged some final words. Then she walked to her car. Frank and Joe watched the two cars drive off in opposite directions.

"So," Frank said. "They both think Lamont's a great guy."

"That's got to be the most harmless conversation I've ever eavesdropped on," Joe said. He tossed his headset to the back of the van, and Frank did the same.

"Two more suspects crossed off our ever shrinking list," Frank said, coiling up the microphone cable.

Joe grunted and put the mike back into its case. "Let's go home," he said.

Late that evening, Joe and Frank sat with Callie and Iola at Mr. Pizza. Their table was dominated by an extra-large Killer Pizza, the specialty of their friend, Tony Prito.

"How did the float turn out?" Frank asked, preparing to bite into a slice of pizza.

"Great," Callie said. "We used over one thousand azaleas."

"I can't even imagine what a thousand azaleas look like all in one place," Joe said.

"It won't make the *Guinness Book of World Records,*" Callie said, "but it's a pretty impressive sight. You'll see it on Sunday."

"How about you two?" Iola asked. "Did you

finish taping? And have you found out who's behind that whole sabotage thing?"

"We've finished taping, but not editing," Frank said. "The news crew will tape the fireworks show itself, and we'll use some of their footage."

"And the only new information we have about possible trouble is all bad. We watched two prime suspects go up in smoke earlier this evening."

When they had finished eating, Frank, Joe, Callie, and Iola piled into Mrs. Hardy's station wagon, which the boys had borrowed for the night. Joe drove past the marina on the way to Callie's house. "Look," Callie said. "There's the *Barbary Blood.* It looks like something from a storybook, doesn't it?"

"I guess it does," Joe said. "Let's hope the story has a happy ending."

After they drove the girls home, Frank and Joe headed for home themselves. They sat in the living room, talking quietly so they wouldn't wake anyone.

"We've got no suspects, a couple of suspicious incidents, and a note." Frank summed up the case. "It all adds up to the possibility of big trouble at the fireworks show. Maybe we should try to get it cancelled—or postponed, at least, until Sunday evening."

"Who'd listen to us?" Joe asked. "Con Riley is annoyed enough at our Lamont theory. And can you see Chief Collig cancelling one of Bayport's biggest tourist attractions on our say-so? The town supervisor would have his head."

"We need hard facts." Frank gave a huge yawn. "And I need some sleep." He looked very glum. "And we still have to edit our report. It's running way too long—fixing it will take a big chunk out of tomorrow."

Joe nodded. "I don't think our investigation would make a good excuse for not finishing what we promised to do. Mona will dance on our heads if we leave her with seven minutes to fill on Monday. She is one producer who doesn't fool around. I'll go down to the station with you tomorrow morning. Maybe with the two of us working, we'll get it done way ahead of deadline."

"Deadline." Frank shuddered. "I don't like the sound of that word." He yawned again. "I'm ready for bed. Maybe the answer to our problems will come to me in a dream."

In a way, it did.

All night, Frank kept reliving the scene where the injured Clinton Lamont took his arm and tried to tell him something. He kept watching those lips, with no sound coming out.

The next morning, when Joe came down to the kitchen, he found Frank already up and making breakfast. "What got you up so early?" he asked.

"A lousy night's sleep," Frank answered,

rubbing his eyes. "It was weird. I kept waking up after the same dream, over and over. There I am, back at Old Glory, where the paramedics are taking Lamont out on the stretcher. He takes my arm and tries to talk to me. I can see his lips move, but no sound comes out. It was like a film loop, running again and again and again."

He forked over some slightly burnt scrambled eggs onto Joe's plate. "Let's finish breakfast and get down to the station. It's going to be a long day."

Twenty minutes later they got into the van and drove to the WBPT building. The guard was a little surprised to see them arrive so early, but Frank's pass was in order, and he let them in. They headed straight for the editing rooms.

That was the last part of the day that went well. After assembling the rough cut Frank had prepared, they had fourteen minutes of good tape footage. They could only have four. Where could they lose ten minutes?

They spent hours trying to cut and condense the information they'd gathered. The shot of the explosive stars in Joe's hand stayed in, with a ten-second voice-over by Frank explaining what they were. They made a montage of quick shots to cover a lot of scenes in the factory. A scene that would be seconds on the screen took an hour to prepare.

Frank's lack of sleep didn't help. He was dull

at the editing board, moving a little too slowly at the buttons when he should have been cutting things by the split second. They had to go over things again and again. And as Frank watched the hands of the clock creep around and around, he thought he was going to explode with frustration. Here he was, doing a gee-whiz story about fireworks while a potential tragedy came closer and closer.

"Maybe we ought to call the folks and tell them not to go to the show tonight," he said as the job went into the late afternoon. "Callie and Iola, too."

Joe looked at him. "I know how you feel," he said. "Let's get this job done, then tackle that one."

It was almost six o'clock when they finally had their show ready. It was four minutes long, right on the nose, with three minutes left open for clips of the fireworks display—if that went as planned.

Frank turned down the sound, just letting the pictures run before his eyes. There he was with the microphone, speaking, his lips silently moving. Suddenly he stood up, left the editing complex, and headed for the newsroom.

Frank opened the closet where recent news tapes were stored. He found the tapes covering the most recent Old Glory incident. Then he and Joe ran through these tapes, looking for the shot of Lamont being carried out of the building.

"Got it!" Joe said, after a twenty-minute search.

"Good," Frank said, moving his chair over to Joe's monitor. "Now take a look at this."

The monitor showed a close-up of Denise Fergus talking directly into the camera, though the sound was turned down. In the background, the two paramedics were coming out of the building carrying the stretcher.

Frank hit the fast-forward button to speed the picture up to the point where Denise asked her question. When it reached that point, he pressed the slow button. Now the image began to move in tiny stages, so that the people on the screen looked like mechanical figures imitating human movements.

Joe and Frank stared at the screen, watching Frank move slowly, slowly toward Lamont on the stretcher. They both mouthed the words, "You were right," along with Lamont's silent lip movements. They watched as Frank leaned over and whispered into Lamont's ear. Then Frank moved away from the camera shot as Lamont tried to say one last thing.

"Here it is," Frank said. "Watch carefully."

Lamont's lips came together. The boys copied his slow, slow lip movements. Together, they both said out loud, "Mmmm-unn-derrr."

12 Collins Comes Clean

Frank stopped the tape. He and Joe looked at each other. "It makes a certain kind of horrible sense," Frank said.

"Sure," Joe agreed. "Who was it that gave us all those helpful suggestions?"

"And every one of them turned out to be misleading, at the very least," Frank said.

"Something tells me that this time we've hit pay dirt," Joe said.

"Let's see what we know about him," Frank said. "He knows his way around the plant as well as anyone else."

"He seems afraid of Lamont," Joe added.

"He's in research and development," Frank said, "so the technical information about fireworks is at his fingertips."

"And he'd probably find it pretty easy to

make off with the ingredients for thermite, or even a little potassium chlorate."

Frank ran the videotape back. "I'll play it again, just to be sure. Let's see how it looks at regular speed."

Frank rewound the tape and ran it again, still with the sound turned down. Once again, they watched Frank lean over, then move aside from the camera shot.

Again, they watched Lamont's lip movements, this time at normal speed. Again, there was no doubt about what he was trying to say. "Munder" was the silent message Lamont had so desperately wanted to pass along to Frank.

"Okay," Joe said. "Let's review what we know. Then maybe we can decide on what we can do."

"We know that Munder broke into Lamont's office," Frank said. "And that he set up the booby trap that sent Lamont to the hospital."

"True," Joe said. "We also know that Munder has tried to throw suspicion on several people other than himself."

"And we know there's going to be a sabotage attempt tonight," Frank added.

"Hold on," Joe said. "Let's think about this for a minute. Do we really know that for a fact?"

"Well," Frank said, "we've got a note, and Munder did feed us a lot of rumors and suspicions. Of course, now it would probably be a good idea not to trust anything Munder has told us."

"On the other hand," Joe pointed out, "Lamont said we were right. I mean, he grabbed your arm after he got hurt. And he seemed to be talking about our sabotage theory."

"Right," Frank said. "And don't forget the note we got last week."

"That note is even more puzzling now than it was then," Joe said. "Who do you think sent it to us?"

"I don't know," Frank said. "Somebody who knew about Munder and wanted to stop him, but couldn't come out publicly." He shoved his hands in his pockets, shaking his head in frustration. "That doesn't describe anyone I know."

Frank rewound the news tape and took it out of the VCR. Then he returned all the tapes to the cabinet.

"Let's go out to the factory and take another look," Frank said. "With Lamont out of the picture, Munder may feel free to monkey with that fireworks stockpile again. We might find something there that can help us stop him."

"I hope we don't have any trouble with Lew Collins," Joe said, following Frank out the door.

"I doubt it," Frank said. "Especially now

that we can tell him that Lamont realized we were on the right track."

At the Old Glory gate, the guard called Collins to ask if the Hardy van was to be allowed on the premises. He hung up and told Frank to drive to the main building, where Collins would meet them.

To their surprise, Collins was standing outside the entrance when they drove up. "He seems pretty anxious to see us," Joe said.

They parked the van, got out, and walked over to where Lew Collins stood. Lamont's assistant looked pale and tired.

"Hey," Frank said. "You look as though you've been working hard. Are the preparations for the celebration getting to you?"

Collins ignored the question. He said, "I hope you two have figured out by now who's planning trouble for tonight."

Frank and Joe looked surprised. Joe said, "You know about Munder, then?"

"I've known about Munder longer than you have," Collins said. "I discovered weeks ago that explosive material was disappearing. I traced it to Munder and found it had something to do with the annual fireworks show. He's the one who took the file on our security plan for the show—the plan that Anna Siegel found and got fired for."

Collins shook his head. "I didn't know just

what Munder had in mind. In fact, I still don't."

"Did you tell Lamont?" Joe asked.

"I—I couldn't," Collins said. "Look, I'm not very proud of what I'm about to tell you. But I have to get it off my chest. Munder had something on me from my last job. They let me go after I had fouled up a big security job—and I lied about it on my application here."

"So, if you told Lamont, Munder threatened to deny everything *and* get you fired," Joe said.

"And the longer I kept my mouth shut, the worse it would look." Collins hung his head. "Munder was really tightening the screws. That's why he vandalized the offices on my shift, to get me in trouble. Even so, Lamont was getting suspicious of him. I think that's why Munder pulled that booby-trap bit."

"And you still did nothing," Frank said.

"Well," Collins said, "I didn't exactly do nothing. I had you guys on the case."

Joe stared. "You mean—*you're* the one who sent us that note!"

"Right," Collins said. "I knew about you and your Crimestoppers bit. I figured if I got you started, you guys could nail Munder without involving me."

"Why didn't you tell us in the note who we were supposed to be investigating?" Frank asked.

"I didn't want you to go straight to Munder," Collins said. "If you had, he'd have known I was the one who'd tipped you off. I had to let you discover him on your own."

"We almost didn't make it in time," Joe said.

"But we did make it," Frank said. "Now, where is he, and where are the fireworks?"

"Most of the stuff is already out at the marina," Lew Collins said. "After the vandalization of Lamont's office, I had three men go over the fireworks with a fine-tooth comb. There's nothing wrong with them. And there's one load left to go—mainly shells and rockets. I'm keeping that in a storage bunker until we have to move it."

"We'll go and check it out," Joe said. "Then we'll meet you at the marina."

"Okay," Collins said. "I'll see you later."

"Sure thing."

Joe and Frank walked quickly toward the storage area. A truck stood by one of the bunkers dug into the earth. "That must be the one we want," Joe said.

Joe took the stairs into the dugout two at a time, with Frank following close behind him. Then they stood in front of the crates of fireworks that would be used in the Founders' Day celebration.

"What are we looking for?" Frank asked.

"Beats me," Joe said.

They walked through the rows of crates, all filled with explosives and rocket nose cones. One set of crates held the specially altered artillery shells which would push the fireworks high into the air. Red light bulbs threw an eerie glow around the room.

"I don't see anything unusual," Joe said. "I just wish we knew what we were looking for."

"We're looking for anything that Munder might have planted in these boxes. If he's put something here, we'll find it. And when we find it, we'll know what his plan is."

They heard a scraping sound behind them. Both boys turned quickly. A figure was standing in the shadows, between them and the door.

"You won't find anything here," a quiet voice told them. "My plan is much more elegant than you seem to think."

Don Munder stepped out of the shadows. The pistol in his hand was aimed right at Frank's face.

"Don't try anything foolish," Munder warned. "Make one move and you're dead."

13 Mad for Revenge

"I guess I should compliment you boys," Munder said, stepping toward them. "I thought I'd thrown you off my trail. In fact, I was sure I hadn't left a trail at all. But then, I was sure the thermite and the potassium chlorate would scare you off. You certainly have guts, you two."

He took a step in their direction. Instinctively, Frank and Joe backed up. They only managed two steps, however, when they reached the wall.

Munder stopped moving toward them. "The light isn't very good in here," he said. "But I'd swear that's fear I see in your faces."

Joe said, "Looking at a gun from this angle tends to do that to us."

"I guess it would," Munder said. "But this is only for my protection. If you do as I say, I have no intention of using the gun. Now that I've got you, I'm going to use you two as a postscript to my plan."

"I'm glad to hear that," Frank said. "I guess you have more sense than to want to face a murder charge."

Munder laughed loudly, and it was a very unpleasant sound.

"Let me tell you how funny that is," he said, getting control of himself. "Before tonight's celebration is over, I'll hold one of the world's records for murder."

"What are you talking about?" Joe asked.

"You two were on the trail all this time," Munder said, "and you never had any idea just how big my plan really was. Tonight, you'll see more destruction than you've ever dreamed of. All the officials of Old Glory, who will be proudly taking part in the festivities; all of Bayport's elected officials, who will be making their annual vote-for-me speeches; and a good number of the thousands of gawkers who will be there to see the fireworks. They'll get more than they expected."

"What are you planning?" Frank asked, his voice dry and rasping.

"I'm going to blow the whole marina!" Munder said, laughing wildly.

Frank and Joe looked at each other, then at the narrow passageway between them and Munder. There was no way either of them could try anything—not with that gun staring them down.

"Now," Munder said, "I want you two to come out this way, with your hands raised far above your heads." He began backing out of the aisle of boxes.

When he reached the end of the aisle, Munder kept backing up until the Hardys were out in the open with him.

"Now," he said, "walk down that ramp. I'll be right behind you, so don't think about getting cute. Just keep walking until you reach that metal closet up ahead."

Joe and Frank did exactly as he said. Though they were silent, they both shared one key thought. Munder wasn't going to kill them. If they went along with him, they might learn his plan—and live to stop him.

"Stop right there!" Munder said as they reached the metal closet. "And keep those hands up!"

Joe and Frank stopped. Munder kept them covered from about ten feet away—too far for them to jump him. Then he said, "Now, Frank, lower your left hand very, very slowly. That's good. Now open the closet door. You see the ropes in there?"

"Yeah," Frank said, looking at two coils of rope on the floor of the closet.

"Good," Munder said. "Take one coil out and put it on your brother's shoulder. Then you take the other one."

Moments later, Munder marched them at gunpoint down another aisle, to a thick metal door. "Inside," Munder said.

The room was windowless, its walls made of raw earth. Munder stood in the doorway, still covering them. "This is extra storage space. It's empty now, and no one will notice that the door is closed when they come to pick up this load. Collins has all the workers down at the marina, going over the stuff that's already been sent."

"What's going on, Munder?" Frank said. "Just what do you have in mind?"

"I've already told you what I have in mind," he said. "And now you two are going to see to it that I get credit for what happens. Lie down on the floor, Frank."

Frank lowered himself to the floor and stretched his legs out.

"No," Munder said. "On your stomach."

Frank rolled over. "How are we going to see that you get credit?" he asked.

"Joe," Munder said, "take one of those ropes and tie him up. I want his feet securely bound, then his hands tied behind his back."

Munder watched Joe tie his brother up. Then he said, "You two will tell the world just what my plan was, and how I carried it out. It's an honor, boys. I wouldn't trust most television people."

Meaning, he was able to string us along—so

he trusts the two dumb kids, Frank thought. "Why are you doing this, Munder?" he asked.

Munder went from cheerful to sad, as if someone had thrown a switch. "You two might understand my motives better than most people. I had a brother. He used to work here. Seven years ago, he was killed during preparations for the Founders' Day festivities."

Joe turned and looked up at Munder. "I remember that," he said. "There was an accident in a storage shed—"

Munder's lip curled. "'Accident,' they said. 'Very sad,' they said." His eyes glittered. "This company killed my brother. They knew they'd done wrong. That's why they moved the factory out here, with all these storage bunkers. For safety." His voice rose to a scream. "But what about my brother's safety? Lamont is Mr. Safe now, but he wasn't when my brother died."

Again, he abruptly shifted moods. Now he was icy cold. "Originally, I planned for him to go up with all the others, at the beginning of tonight's display. But he was suspicious of me—so I had to get him out of the way. Too bad I had to hurry—that booby trap should have done the job."

Joe stood up, having tied Frank's hands and feet. "So you're doing this because of what happened to your brother," Joe said. "Doesn't it all seem kind of pointless? What you're about to do won't bring him back."

Munder didn't even seem to hear. "Take that other rope," he said, "and tie your feet together." Joe obeyed.

Then Munder swung into another mood. "I know it won't bring him back, you fool! I realized the moment it happened that nothing would ever bring him back. But from that moment on, there's been only one thing that I've wanted. Revenge! I'm going to show them all that they can't get away with what they did to my brother."

Joe had finished tying his own feet together. Munder motioned for him to lie on his stomach next to Frank. Then he reached down and checked the rope around Joe's feet. When he was satisfied that it was tight enough, he put the gun down, out of Joe's reach.

Then he set about tying Joe's hands behind his back. When that was done, he took out a knife and cut two long lengths of rope. He used one to tie a noose around Frank's neck. Then he tied the other end around the ropes securing Frank's feet. He repeated the process with Joe.

"This should keep you pretty much immobile," he said. "Every time you struggle, it will tighten the noose on your neck. Struggle hard enough, and you're likely to strangle yourselves to death."

"But you still haven't told us what you'll be doing, Munder," Frank said. "Will you swim out to the *Barbary Blood* and throw a lighted match on it?"

Munder seemed to find that very funny. Then he cut off in midlaugh. "No, a lighted match wouldn't do it. I won't even be on the scene. I'm going to set this explosion off by means of a radio transmitter. When you tell the story to the police and the press, I'd like you to mention that I invented this particular transmitter."

"What are you talking about?" Joe said.

"It will happen just when the town supervisor and his gang arrive. That should be about fifteen minutes before the show should begin. When he steps up to the microphones, I'll hit this little button." Munder pulled a transmitter box from his pocket. It had a red button in its center.

"This will detonate the bomb I've placed in the main hatch cover on the *Barbary Blood*'s deck—right where they're piling the shells for the fireworks mortars." Hc smilcd thinly. "I calculate the ship, the dais, the marina, and the three blocks closest to the water should go up."

He gave a tug to the ropes binding Frank's hands and feet. Then he did the same with Joe's ropes.

"Now you know everything," he said. "It's too bad that you won't be there to see all the fireworks. But if you were, you'd never be around to give me the credit, would you?"

Munder took a handkerchief from his pocket, tore it in two, and stuffed one half into Joe's mouth, the other into Frank's mouth. Then he stood up and surveyed his work. "I think that should keep you two. Don't worry—before I sail off, I'll call and tell the police where you are. By the time they rescue you, I'll be long gone."

He stopped in the doorway. "Remember, boys, I let you live when I didn't have to. You owe me one. And you'll repay me by simply telling the truth to the press and the police."

The thick metal door clanged shut. Frank and Joe couldn't even hear Munder's footsteps as he left.

14 Goodbye, Bayport

Frank and Joe immediately started trying to spit out their gags. Escape would be much simpler if they could talk about what they were doing.

Munder didn't really expect them to be heard in the soundproof room. He hadn't even tied the gags in place. Soon, both Frank and Joe had a loose tail of cloth sticking out of their mouths.

Joe wriggled and slid, until Frank's tied hands were an inch from the loose corner of his gag. Frank fumbled, managed to grab the cloth with his fingers, and Joe slowly moved his head back.

"Boy, that thing tastes awful!" Joe said. "Let's take care of yours now."

They both wriggled and slid until they were

face-to-face. The loose cloth hung near Frank's chin. Joe grabbed it in his teeth, and they both moved their heads back.

Frank let out a sigh of relief. "Well," he said, "now we can talk. Next step—how do we get out of here?"

He tried to shift around, and nearly choked. "This rope around my neck was a cute idea. I can't move my arms or my legs without closing off my windpipe."

"Let me do the moving," Joe said. "My noose seems to be looser than yours."

He inched toward a set of steel closets in one corner. Then he started a series of two-footed kicks against one of the closet doors.

"What are you doing?" Frank asked.

"Kicking," Joe said, his face turning red as his own noose began to cut into his throat. "And praying that my guess is correct—that there are some tools in there to help us."

He gave another kick, and the door swung open. He could see only the bottom two shelves inside.

"Tape," he said. "Tape and paper. That isn't going to get us out of here."

Slowly he moved to the next closet and kicked again. The door opened immediately to show empty shelves.

"Don't panic," Joe said to his brother. "I still have six more closets to inspect."

Frank's answer was a gasp. However he

moved, the noose cut deeper into his throat, strangling him.

Joe moved to the next closet. He opened it in three kicks. "Hold on, Frank, there's a chisel on the bottom shelf."

Joe managed to scrape the chisel along with his bound feet, grunting with the effort. Frank felt as if the rope around his neck were sawing through his Adam's apple. Black dots danced before his eyes as he watched Joe grab the chisel and worm his way back.

"Can you get on your side?" Joe asked. "This won't be easy."

Feeling as if he were pushing a mountain, Frank managed to roll over. Joe began stabbing at the rope with the chisel. For Frank, everything was getting hazy . . . and then the rope popped, the noose loosened, and Frank gulped in fresh air.

"I feel as though I've been set free," he said.

"Not quite yet," Joe pointed out. "Now you can get to work on my noose. Then I'll get your hands free. After that, it will be all downhill."

When Frank finally got his hands loose, he checked his watch—nearly an hour had passed. They had only forty-five minutes to stop Munder. He frantically freed Joe's hands, then went to work on the ropes on his legs. "Let's get out of here."

They bounded out of the storeroom and up the stairs, then ran at top speed to the van. The whole plant area was eerily silent. "Everybody must be down at the marina," Frank said. "That's where we've got to get, fast!"

Ten minutes later, Frank edged the van into a side street about a mile from the marina. Last-minute fireworks fans had the streets completely blocked.

"Park the van," Joe said. "We'll run the rest of the way."

Frank pulled the van to the curb, in a space clearly marked No Parking. "Who pays for the parking ticket?" he asked as they jumped out.

"If we stop Munder," Joe said, "the town supervisor will give us a pardon." He and Frank began running in the direction of the marina.

"If we don't," Frank said, "there won't be any town."

The closer they got to the marina, the thicker the crowds became. That made it harder and harder for them to move fast. It took the boys much longer to reach the bay than any other mile they'd ever run.

A boat shuttled back and forth from the *Barbary Blood* to one of the marina piers. The boys shoved their way through the crowd until they came to the blocked-off entrance. Three private security types stood guard, while Lew Collins stood by, a pair of binoculars in his hands.

"Lew!" Frank said, running to the edge of the gate.

Collins looked up. "What are you—" Then he saw the look on Frank's face. "It's Munder, isn't it?" he asked, throwing open the gate.

"He's hidden a bomb in the main hatch cover on the *Barbary Blood,*" Frank said. "It's radio-controlled, and it goes off when the town supervisor arrives to give his speech."

Collins hustled the Hardys to the end of the pier, where an older man was climbing into the shuttle boat. "Hold it for us!" Collins cried.

They jumped aboard, and Collins started for the pirate ship at top speed. "Bert Sawyer, meet the Hardy brothers—Frank and Joe." Collins looked over at the older man. "This may be a lucky break. You were a demolitions man in the army, weren't you?"

"I did some bomb work, yes," Sawyer said.

"That's good. Because there's a bomb planted under the main hold hatch of the *Barbary Blood.*"

For a second, Sawyer laughed. Nobody else joined in. His face grew pale. "You're serious, aren't you?" he said softly.

"Deadly serious, Mr. Sawyer," Joe said.

"It's not possible," Sawyer said. "The ship has been guarded carefully ever since it was towed into the bay. Who would have put a bomb on it?"

"Don Munder," Frank said. "Never mind why. The bomb is there. Munder is around here somewhere with a transmitter, and he's going to blow the whole marina sky-high if you don't get that bomb defused."

Sawyer's eyes went wide in alarm. Then he reached down, picked up a mike, and spoke into it, never taking his eyes from Frank and Joe.

"Tim?" He said. "Tim, this is Bert. Come in, Tim."

"What's up, Bert?" said a voice that crackled from the speaker inside the boat.

"Tim," Sawyer said, "I want you to take a look under the main hatch cover of the ship."

"Hatch cover? Bert, I'm pretty busy here, I haven't got time—"

"Look at it!" Bert yelled. "Look under that cover, and see if you find anything there."

"Check," Tim said. "Hold on."

Sawyer didn't say a word as they waited. Tim was back on the line in about thirty seconds.

"Bert?" he said.

"Yeah."

"There is something there—a box, freshly nailed into the wood. Should I open it?"

"Don't touch it!" Bert said. "I'll be out to deal with it. And, Tim—get the life rafts ready—quietly."

He began rubbing his hands together nervously as they came closer to the boat. Collins pulled up the shuttle boat right by a rope ladder leading to the deck of the *Barbary Blood.* Bert Sawyer climbed up, closely followed by Joe. When Collins went to follow,

Frank took his arm. "We still have another job," he said. "We've got to find Munder!"

Frank took the binoculars from around the security man's neck and pointed them toward the end of the bay. "Munder said he'd be escaping by boat. And those piers over there are the only ones that wouldn't be touched by the blast." Collins started up the engines as Frank began scanning the docks.

Sawyer and Joe climbed onto the deck. Joe followed Sawyer over to the main hatch.

A confused-looking younger man had the hatch cover levered up, revealing the box he'd described. Sawyer grabbed a toolbox and slid himself under the hatch cover.

Joe stared at the piles of artillery shells stacked around on the deck. "Can you defuse it, Mr. Sawyer?" he asked shakily.

"It's been years," Sawyer muttered. "But I don't see that I have any choice. I at least have to give it a try."

As the shuttle boat sped across Barmet Bay, Frank swung his binoculars back and forth. Back at the marina, he saw the crowds turning into one huge mass as the time for the fireworks show approached. He saw the police cars cut a line through the crowd, though he couldn't hear their sirens. He saw the town supervisor's limousine follow the police cars to the speakers' platform.

The platform itself was filled with executives

of Old Glory and a handful of Bayport's elected officials. This was the crowd Munder was after.

Frank swung back to the smaller, out-of-the-way piers where he and Collins were headed. There was a small crowd there—Frank realized that in some ways they'd have a better view. The pirate ship was lit up from behind by the lights of Bayport. Perhaps, next year—if there was a Founders' Day next year . . .

The shuttle boat was close enough now that he could make out all the details of the handful of ships moored at the pier. He thought he saw someone moving on the deck of an old cabin cruiser.

It was Munder, with his own set of binoculars. For a second, they seemed to stare at each other. Had he recognized him and Collins? Munder's attention seemed to be riveted to the platform on the other side of the bay.

Frank focused back there in time to see the town supervisor climbing the steps to the platform.

The supervisor stood at the head of the platform, ready to address the crowd. Frank swung back to Munder to find the man raising his transmitter box, his thumb over the red button in the center.

Frank drew a sharp breath. "Goodbye, Bayport."

With a wild smile, Munder jabbed the button.

15 Fireworks

The booming echo of the loudspeakers across the bay came across the water. "My friends," the town supervisor said, "I'm happy to welcome you . . ."

Through his binoculars, Frank watched Munder gawk, shake his transmitter box, and press the red button again and again. Nothing happened. Munder threw the transmitter to the deck of the cabin cruiser and looked around wildly.

On the deck of the *Barbary Blood,* Sawyer slid out from under the hatch cover, sweat pouring down his face, a pair of wire cutters in his hand. At the sound of the town supervisor's voice coming over the loudspeaker, Joe let out the breath he'd been holding.

"Looks like you cut the right wire, Mr. Sawyer," he said.

The area was full of Old Glory workers, who

now knew what all the commotion had been about. They gave Sawyer a loud cheer as he stood up on deck.

Sawyer basked in the cheer for about five seconds. Then he said, "Okay, guys. Back to work. We have a fireworks show to put on."

As the crew leapt to work, Sawyer turned to Joe. "Sorry I doubted you," he said. "But it did sound a little weird."

"Forget it," Joe said. "We're all just lucky that you knew what to do."

"This ship is loaded with people who could have done it," Sawyer said. "I just didn't have time to interview people for their qualifications. By the way, where did your brother go?"

"I don't know," Joe said. "He and Collins swung away in the boat—I guess they're going to find Munder."

"I've known Don Munder for years," Sawyer said. "I can't believe he'd do a thing like this."

"Believe it," Joe said.

Collins jockeyed the shuttle boat to block the prow of Munder's cabin cruiser. He jumped down onto the pier while Frank climbed onto the nose of the other craft. They'd decided to come at Munder from two different directions.

As he crept along the foredeck, Frank could see through the windshield into the ship's cockpit. The whole ship was vibrating as its engines throbbed. But the cockpit was empty.

Then a figure appeared behind the wheel—Lew Collins. As he reached for the controls to kill the engine, another figure appeared behind him.

Frank didn't even have a chance to yell a warning before Munder coldcocked Collins with his pistol butt. The security man dropped to the deck, stunned.

Then Munder pointed the pistol at Frank through the windshield. "Why don't you come in, Mr. Hardy?"

Frank had no choice. He entered the cockpit. "I thought that was you out there, but I couldn't believe it." Munder's voice was polite, but so brittle it sounded as if it would crack. A slight tremor in his hand made the gun weave ever so little.

"I guess I should have believed it," Munder went on. "You and your brother have certainly given me a major problem."

"Things didn't go according to plan, did they?" Frank said.

"Not exactly," Munder said. "But all is not lost."

"Meaning what?"

"I have a store of explosives right here with me," Munder said. "I'm going to ram the pirate ship. I'll get the job done, even if I have to die to do it."

"You won't make it," Frank told him. "Collins has already radioed the harbor police.

They know what your boat looks like. And they won't let you near the *Barbary Blood.*"

"I'll just have to race them, then," Munder said. "But I don't have any choice. Those people must pay for my brother's death. Now, get away from that doorway."

Munder reached over to undo the line that held the boat to the dock. As the boat began to move, Frank saw his chance.

He kicked at Munder's hand, sending the gun splashing into the water. Then he lunged at Munder.

But Munder kicked as well, sending Frank reeling back into the steering wheel. Munder jumped on him, dragging him to the deck. The boat pitched wildly, moving faster and faster, but Frank had no idea in which direction they were now headed.

Munder tried to choke Frank, but Frank got a hand under the man's chin and pushed him off. Munder fell backward, and Frank quickly got to his feet.

Flailing around, Munder's hand touched a fishing rod. He grabbed it and whipped it out toward Frank's face. Frank dodged, the barbed hook at the end of the line scratching a thin line along his cheek, just under the eye. Munder then tried to use the rod as a club, but now Frank was too close. The rod whistled over his head.

Frank crashed into Munder, ramming him back into the built-in chairs at the rear of the cockpit. They rolled across the deck, neither able to get the upper hand.

Frank reared up on his knees to punch Munder, but the boat lurched again, throwing him against the unconscious form of Lew Collins. Munder squirmed free, pulling himself up on the wheel. He laughed wildly as he looked through the windscreen.

A huge, dark bulk rose up in front of them, brightly lit from the rear. The *Barbary Blood!*

The wail of sirens cut across the water—the harbor police were obviously closing in. But would they be in time?

Munder's eyes were glued to the pirate ship. He grabbed the wheel with one hand and the throttle with the other, preparing for his suicide attack. "You're not going to stop me, Hardy," he said through clenched teeth. "I *will* blow up that ship. Why don't you just let it happen?"

Frank tackled the man, forcing him down to the deck. But Munder's hand stayed clenched to the throttle. The cabin cruiser bolted forward. They were so close to the *Barbary Blood* now that its hull cut off the light from the marina.

Desperately, Frank broke Munder's hold, throwing the man on his back. He raised his right arm high, then brought it down on Munder's face.

Munder went limp. Frank didn't even wait to see if he'd knocked him out. He jumped for the steering wheel, throttling down. He was close enough to see Bert Sawyer's face staring down at him from the rail of the *Barbary Blood.* The two ships' hulls nearly scraped as Frank turned the cabin cruiser away.

A pair of police launches came at him from either side, sirens blaring. Frank recognized Con Riley and Chief Collig on one of them. A third boat joined them, with Joe Hardy aboard. Frank cut the cabin cruiser's engine.

Down by his feet, Frank heard a pair of groans. Lew Collins and Don Munder were both coming around just as the harbor police climbed aboard.

Joe leapt onto the cabin cruiser's deck. "You okay, Frank?"

"Just fine," Frank said. "Now that all the excitement's over."

Con Riley came aboard. "I suppose you two have a full explanation for all this," he said, smiling.

"We have." Frank pointed at Munder. "There's your bombmaker."

Con looked down at Munder, who was sitting up on the deck, holding a hand to his face. Con briskly put handcuffs on him.

"You know," Con said, "I think Lamont was right about you two. You not only report the news, you go around making it as well."

"You're reminding me we've got a job to do," Frank said, turning to Joe. "How are things on the ship? Do we have an end to our feature?"

His answer was a dull *boom!*

Then a spear of white light lanced upward as the first skyrocket hissed into the dark sky.

Joe glanced at his watch. "Looks like we've got an ending all right," he said. "And right on time."